Saving the Boxer

Neil S. Plakcy

Copyright 2023 Neil S. Plakcy

This romance novel is a work of fiction. Names, characters, places, and incidents either are products of the author's imagination or are used fictitiously. Any resemblance to actual events or locales or persons, living or dead, is entirely coincidental. All rights reserved, including the right of reproduction in whole or in part in any form.

NO AI TRAINING: Without in any way limiting the author's [and publisher's] exclusive rights under copyright, any use of this publication to "train" generative artificial intelligence (AI) technologies to generate text is expressly prohibited. The author reserves all rights to license uses of this work for generative AI training and development of machine learning language models.

Chapter 1

The Sailor and the Boxer

Silas

Silas Warner was immediately taken by the look of the dark-skinned man across the bar. He had coal-black hair and skin that looked as smooth as silk, as well as a wiry mustache and beard. His dark blue jacket had brass buttons, but had seen better days, as had his white shirt, which was frayed around the collar.

He picked up his glass of ale and worked his way across the crowded room. He was surprised that the handsome man was by himself in this bar where men came to meet others of similar outlook.

Silas had to deflect overtures from two different men on his way. If the fellows were so eager, what kept them away from the object of his interest? Was it the darkness of his skin? He was clearly from India, and had the look of a sailor about him, from his roughened hands to his stiff posture.

Silas had no prejudices. He loved cock, and variety of cock even more. The sailor intrigued him, and as he got closer his interest grew, stiffening his stand. He smiled as he caught the sailor's eye, and was rewarded with a smile in return.

"I haven't seen you here before," Silas said. It was a weak opening, he knew, but it was the best he could come up with after a full glass of ale.

"I arrived only yesterday on the Maharana," he said. "A merchant ship out of Bombay, with a load of Indian silks and crates of tea from the highlands."

"Bombay," Silas said with a breath. "Is it as beautiful as they say?"

"It is," the Indian said. "Elegant domed temples built of yellow basalt, palatial homes with hidden gardens full of beautiful scented flowers."

"Do you miss it?"

"It is my heart and my home," the man said. "But there is little work for me there, so I sail the seas to earn my keep and return when I can."

He nodded to Silas. "And what of you? Where are you from?"

"Originally from Sheffield, in the north," he said. "But when my father discovered my nature, he drove me away. Now I have a room a few blocks from here."

The man nodded. "It was necessary for me to leave my home as well." He held out his hand. "I am Raj."

"Silas," he said. The man's hand was rough but strong.

"I have been to London several times," Raj said. "I have seen all the major sights. But I haven't seen your room. Would you like to show it to me?"

Silas laughed. He drained his glass and tugged on Raj's hand. "Follow me."

The bar's main advantage, to Silas at least, was its proximity to his room on Bryanston Mews West. He laughed as they exited the bar, excited by the thought of a new conquest, and an exotic one at that.

"Are you always so forward with the men you meet?" Silas asked as they hurried down the pavement.

"As you saw in the bar, I am not to everyone's taste," Raj said. "So when I find a man I like, who likes me, why waste time?"

"Why, indeed!" They reached the boarding house and Silas unlocked the front door and led Raj upstairs.

"I like the colors of your room," Raj said, when they walked into Silas's bedroom. He had hung brightly colored scarves, some silk and bedazzled with tiny stones, over his bed. "I feel right at home."

They undressed quickly and Silas was happy to see Raj's strong muscles, the result of long labor on board ship. His cock, while not particularly thick, was long and curved at the end and somewhat darker than the rest of his body. His muscular thighs and calves were hairless, and Silas kept rubbing his hands over Raj's smooth back.

With difficulty, he pulled his mouth off Raj's and started kissing his neck and his shoulders. Raj groaned softly as Silas bit lightly at his nipples. Silas licked at his armpits, and then with his tongue he made a trail down Raj's chest.

"You must stop for a moment," Raj said.

Silas pulled back and looked at him. "We must be clean for each other," Raj said. He left Silas's side and crossed the room to where the ewer of water sat on the table. He wet a cloth thoroughly and washed himself—under his arms, along his long cock, then his bollocks. He bent forward slightly and Silas caught his breath as Raj wrapped a slim finger in the worn cloth and worked it up his crack.

It was an unexpectedly erotic vision, made even more so when Raj flipped the cloth over and performed the same service on Silas.

They made love then, slowly and then rapidly, and both of them spent at nearly the same time. Then Raj pulled a watch on a gold chain from his pocket. "Good, we still have time to catch the fights at New Cross."

Silas turned on his side to stare at the naked Indian. "You don't want to stay here?"

"I have many things to do in London and only a few days," he said. "You will come with me?"

"I'm not much for boxing," Silas said. He drew his knees up to his chest and wrapped his arms around them. "But you go if you like."

"Have you ever been?"

Silas shook his head.

"You should not dismiss something you have not experienced," Raj said. "Come, let us get dressed and go. Together." He smiled. "If you like seeing strong men sweating and grappling each other, you will enjoy this."

Silas smiled. "Well, if there will be strong, sweaty men."

Raj treated them to a carriage which took them across the Thames to New Cross. There was already a crowd of men clambering to get in and Silas found he was excited.

The first round did not disappoint him. The opponents were both young, strapping, and blond, farm boys come to the city to make their fortunes. Raj pointed out their inexperience in missed moves and failed punches, and Silas began to understand what he was watching.

The men of the second round were not so attractive, both of them older and more beaten down, though there was a point when they were in a clinch and Silas felt himself getting hard.

He looked around. Did the other men react the same way? He doubted it. They were cheering and yelling instructions at the boxers, waving betting tickets in the air.

It took until the third round for Silas to truly become addicted to the fights. "Now entering the ring, Ezra Curiel, the Hammering Hebrew!" the announcer called, and Silas gasped.

The man before him was almost an Adonis, with finely sculpted muscles, traces of black hair on his arms and legs, and a thick, luxurious pelt on his back. Silas couldn't help staring as he raised his right fist in the air and did a slow circle of the ring. Then their eyes locked, and Curiel smiled.

Silas was sure the smile was directed at him. He watched, drymouthed, as Curiel's opponent was brought into the ring. He was tall and gawky, his only advantages seemingly long legs and long arms. The two touched gloves, and then began to spar.

Silas had forgotten all about Raj by then, so intent was he on Ezra Curiel. To his inexperienced eyes, the man was a masterful boxer, darting back and forth, evading blows from his opponent, who was a hulking lunk in comparison. He couldn't help but feel that Curiel was putting on a show, that he could have despatched the other boxer quickly, but he was entertaining the audience with his elaborate footwork and his glee whenever a punch hit its mark.

The crowd loved him, cheering boisterously. Silas yelled himself hoarse until Curiel delivered the final blow and his opponent fell to the ground.

His chest was matted with sweat and his face dripped, but he hoisted his gloved hands victoriously. And then, before he left the ring, he looked directly at Silas again.

"Are you glad I brought you here?" Raj asked, as the hands prepared the ring for the next bout.

"I am," Silas said. "I never knew there was so much pleasure to be had in such an environment."

"I must leave you here," Raj said. "I have to return to my ship. Will you be able to get back to your room?"

"I am a Londoner now," Silas said. "Don't worry about me."

They exchanged smiles and then Raj disappeared into the crowd.

Silas felt bereft. He'd already witnessed the best boxer he could imagine, so without Raj there was no reason to stay. But still he lingered, finally making his way outside. The air was fetid and muggy but a small cluster of men waited outside the rear door of the arena.

"What are you waiting for?" Silas asked one of the men.

"The boxers come out this way and we cheer for them," the man said. "They'll usually autograph programs if you ask."

Silas looked down at the crumpled program in his hand. Had he realized he might want Curiel's autograph he would have been more careful with it. Then the door opened, and Curiel and two other victors stepped out. The crowd cheered, and clustered around, but Silas waited in the background until all programs had been signed and the audience had disappeared. Curiel was the last left, and Silas walked up to him uncertainly.

Then the boxer smiled. "I was hoping you'd stay around," he said.

Chapter 2

Wine Bar

Ezra

"Are you a lover of the fights?" Ezra asked the man before him, who held a crumpled program in his hand.

"I was not until this evening, and I saw you box," the man said.

Ah, so there had been something in his eye, indeed. Ezra had been careful to keep his two lives separate since his arrival from France. He thought of them as two confining crates, each one he had to fight to escape. He had never responded to another man's overture in either sphere—until now.

"What is your name?" he asked. "And do you have a pen?"

The man stared at him. "Silas," he said. "Silas Warner."

Ezra smiled. The man was truly adorable, with a well-formed body, a shy smile, and floppy blond hair.

"Would you like me to sign your program, Silas Warner?" Ezra asked. "Usually those who want an autograph come with a pen."

"I'm s-sorry," he stuttered, "I didn't think."

"It is all right," Ezra said. "Perhaps you will accompany me for a glass of wine? We could see if we find a pen at the bar."

It was very charming the way Silas's whole face lit up at the invitation. "I would, I would love to," he said. "I'm sorry, I'm not usually so awkward. I am the junior clerk to a barrister at the Inns of Court, and I must speak a great deal. But you—you tie my tongue in knots."

"Perhaps a glass of wine will untangle it," Ezra said. "There is a good wine bar not too far from here in the shadow of the Tower Bridge."

"That's fine. I live in that direction."

"You do? Well, we shall see about that later." He looked around. No one appeared to be paying attention to them, so it was safe to walk off with Silas—as if he was any other fan.

He took Silas's arm by the elbow and steered him out to the street. A breeze swept through, moving some of the fetid air away, and Ezra felt as if he could breathe again, after a long time.

"What is it that you do, as a clerk?" he asked. "I have never had occasion to employ a barrister."

"While Mr. Pemberton argues cases in the court, his clerks are responsible for running his office," Silas said. "I began there two years ago, when the chief clerk left his employ to work in Parliament. Pemberton had at that time a junior clerk, Cyril Alderton, and a boy called Robb who ran errands. Cyril was promoted to senior clerk, and I was able to use my experience and my personal charm to replace Cyril."

He seemed to relax as they walked through Rotherhithe toward the Thames. It was a grim neighborhood of warehouses that supported the port, and at that hour the streets were largely deserted. But Ezra's only fear was that someone might see him with this fey man and understand what they were doing together. That could be more fatal than any blow.

"I am responsible for arranging Mr. Pemberton's diary and general work program," Silas continued. "A good part of my time is spent urging him to get to court, or retrieving him from court to meet with clients. I also copy out documents—I have a beautiful hand, you know."

Ezra smiled. "Yes, your hands are quite beautiful. Unlike mine, which are battered and scarred."

"Not my hand itself," Silas said. "My handwriting."

"Forgive me. I am but an ignorant Frenchman who is still learning your complicated language."

"You speak quite well, for a man who uses his fists rather than his speech. Where did you learn your English? Here in London?"

Ezra shook his head. "The head of my school in Tours had the idea that it was easiest to learn a foreign language as a child. So we had hours of English each week, along with our study of Hebrew."

"Really? You can speak that ancient language?"

"I cannot speak it, only parrot the sounds and read the characters," Ezra said. "That language study was solely in preparation for our ritual called the bar mitzvah, when we are called to read from our scriptures, the Torah, in front of the congregation. When that demonstration is complete, we are said to have reached manhood, and to assume all the responsibilities of the adult male."

They turned onto Tooley Street, heading toward the Tower Bridge. Ezra was confident that with his cap on and his shoulders lowered, no one would recognize him as the Hammering Hebrew, and he could be more himself.

"How fascinating," Silas said. "And do you continue to read that language now?"

Ezra shrugged. "My father relocated us to Paris soon after my bar mitzvah, and we attended services only infrequently. Here in London I attend the Bevis Marks synagogue in Aldgate only for our most important holidays." He smiled. "And because my father threatens me with discipline if I do not."

Silas laughed. "Is your father a boxer, too? That he can discipline a man as strong as you?"

"Parents of Jewish children have a much stronger method than physical power," he said with a smile. "It is called guilt. My father will say things like 'I did not struggle to raise you in our religion only to have you abandon it as an adult.'"

He used a much deeper French accent for his father's words, which Silas found charming.

"'Think of the sacrifices our people have made to bring you to this point,'" Ezra continued. "'We were slaves in Egypt. We were banished from Spain. And for what? So you can play instead of pray on a holiday?'"

They arrived at the wine bar, decked with the French tricolor outside. He'd been there before, accepted as an ordinary Frenchman, and none of the other customers either followed the fights or attended his synagogue, so he could be as anonymous as he wished.

He paused before opening the door and removed his wedding ring from his pocket. He tried to slip it on his finger without Silas noticing, but to no avail.

"You are married," Silas said.

"I would call it a union of mutual benefit rather than a marriage," Ezra said. "But oh, your English language does not have the subtlety of French."

He opened the door. "Now for that wine?"

He was pleased to see that Silas accepted his explanation. They settled at a table in the corner and he ordered a bottle of wine for them to share. "Tell me more about the work of a barrister," he said. "I believe the role is different from that of a solicitor?"

"A solicitor meets with clients, provides them with legal advice, drafts documents, and handles settlements. A barrister is engaged if a client's case requires a court appearance."

Silas then flipped the conversation back to Ezra. "What is the life of a boxer like? Is that all you do? Or do you have another job the rest of the week?"

"I am fortunate that I do not have to maintain other employment," Ezra said. "It took me a while to master my skills and earn a living with my fists, but I manage. It is an itinerant lifestyle to some degree. I am often called on to appear on cards in other cities. I do not ask for, or receive, top billing. But as you will have heard, I have a distinction among boxers."

"The Hammering Hebrew," Silas said.

"Indeed. I was christened thus early in my career. People have an opinion of men of my race as quiet and bookish, and to see a man of my physique and strength is a surprise to them. That distinction has allowed me to travel the length and breadth of the British Isles. Last week, I was in Wales; soon I will box in Newcastle."

They continued to talk, over glasses of the red wine Ezra had ordered them. As a Frenchman, Ezra had a great tolerance for wine. It had been mixed with his water as a child. But sometimes he forgot that Englishmen did not have the same ability. He noticed that Silas was having trouble remaining upright.

He had been a fool, in many ways. Grabbing a man up at the boxing arena with the intent to take him to bed was dangerous. And then he'd allowed the two of them to drink too much wine. "Come along, I shall see you home," Ezra said. He stood and lifted Silas by one arm.

"My home," Silas said, with a goofy grin on his face. "My bed."

"Just home," Ezra said. "I will be lucky if you stay awake long enough to get you there."

He managed to get Silas's address out of him, and then leverage him out of the bar and into the street, where he hailed a carriage. There was no question that he could accompany Silas—who knew who might be watching when they arrived? He gave the driver Silas's address then handed him an extra shilling. "This is for you to get him inside."

"Yes, guv'nor," the driver said.

"Take care of yourself, Silas Warner," Ezra said. "And if the Lord wishes it, we will meet again."

Chapter 3

Wool-Gathering

Silas

When Silas woke up the next morning he was slumped just inside the door to his room. He couldn't remember how he had gotten there, or why he hadn't managed to make it to his bed. He was fully dressed, though, in the same clothes he had worn to the molly bar where he met the sailor the night before.

His head ached like the very devil. He managed to pull himself up and pour a glass of water from the ewer on the table. Once he was able to stand, he warmed up a glass of milk and dropped a spoonful of soot into it. He drank the dismal concoction, then stripped his clothes off and crawled into bed.

His bedding had an unusual scent, and he sniffed carefully. There was the usual smell of tallow soap used by his landlady, mixed in with spend and sweat, and something that reminded him of bay rum. That must have been the sailor.

Once he remembered Raj, the Indian sailor, he recalled accompanying him to the boxing match at New Cross. Then catching the boxer's eye and accompanying him to a wine bar. But after that, all was blank.

It wasn't that he was an easy drunk. He could handle several glasses of ale without any adverse effects. But wine was different.

Had he brought the boxer here? He simply couldn't remember. So he rolled over and went back to sleep.

By the time he had to go to work on Monday, he had recovered his equilibrium, but still couldn't recall how he had gotten home from the wine bar, and whether he'd been alone or not.

His employer, Richard Pemberton, was a barrister at Gray's Inn, one of the four Inns of Court and a mainstay of the British legal profession. Silas walked through the chill October air to Pemberton's office, at the intersection of High Holborn and Gray's Inn Road. He passed the gatehouse and the coat of arms, which always made Silas feel like part of a long line of British jurisprudence.

He bypassed the Great Hall, with its high ceilings, intricate wooden carvings, and large stained-glass window, to head directly for Pemberton's office, on the second floor of a building overlooking the Old Square. As usual, Cyril Alderton was at his desk transcribing notes from Pemberton's rough hand.

Silas hung his coat on a peg and slid into his desk. Pemberton was due in court in an hour, and Silas made sure that all the necessary materials were assembled for him. The boy, Robb, arrived, and was sent on errands, and the day proceeded much as usual, though there were times when a flash of memory would come to Silas.

Catching Ezra Curiel's eye as he prepared for his fight. The feel of Ezra's hand on his arm as they left the arena. Sitting at the wine bar across from Ezra, a glass of red in his hand.

And yet he could not get any farther than that. It was frustrating. Had he bedded the man? Been so worn out by fucking that he'd slumped against his door after Ezra left? How maddening it was to have had such an important evening and then forgotten half of it.

"Silas!"

He looked up to see Cyril standing over him. He wasn't a tall man, but he had a way of pursing his lips and staring at a person. Robb called it his evil eye.

"Yes, Cyril?"

"You've been wool-gathering, boy," Cyril said. "I called you twice from my desk and you did not answer."

"Sorry, Cyril. It's Monday, you know."

"Yes, and you should be fully rested over the weekend so that you can attack your chores on Monday with alacrity. Mr. Pemberton requires this book from the library. Please fetch it as soon as possible."

"Yes, Cyril." Silas took the paper from Cyril and hurried out into the garden. The sun was out and the smog had lifted a bit, and it was a lovely time to be outdoors. Soon London would be bitter cold, besieged by snow and sleet, but for the moment Silas could note the glowing reds, oranges and yellows of the leaves and the last flowers of the season.

The Gray's Inn library held a vast collection of legal literature and historical documents, making it a valuable resource for law students, practitioners, and researchers. One of Silas's first tasks as Pemberton's junior clerk had been to fetch a book from there, and he'd been awed by the vast collection. Now he walked up to the classical brick building with its multipaned windows as if he belonged there—which he did.

He had struggled, in his first year in London, working for a low-level barrister who had few cases of interest and little money to pay. But Silas had worked hard, learning all he could, and then jumped to another barrister, a few steps up the ladder.

He had quickly established Pemberton's office as his goal. Not only was Pemberton well-regarded as a barrister, he had an elegant office and an important clientele. And of greatest interest to Silas was the rumor he heard, that Pemberton was often seen squiring handsome young men around to social events, calling them his "protégés."

Of course, these were usually young men of high birth who were interested in becoming barristers themselves, so Silas did not aspire to become one of them. He was happy simply to work for a man who was a success despite his sexual interests.

His footsteps echoed on the paneled floor as he hurried down the colonnaded walkway, past rows and rows of shelves, until he found the area he needed. He found the book that Pemberton had requested, and then spent some time reviewing nearby volumes until he found two more that related to the same kind of case.

He thought Pemberton would be pleased by that, and the barrister was. "You are coming along quite well, young Silas," he said, when Silas presented him the three books.

Well into his forties, Pemberton was a commanding figure, heavier than he should have been. A few gray hairs nestled amongst the black.

He crossed the room to close the office door gently. "Perhaps you will soon be able to assist Cyril in his copying," he said.

"It would be my honor," Silas said.

"Just between us, have you noticed anything about Cyril's health? He seems to be

flagging to some degree, though he is careful to hide it."

"He is a diligent worker," Silas said. "Though I have noticed that toward the end of the day he needs an extra tea break to keep working."

"He is a good man," Pemberton said. "Keep an eye on him, please?"

"I will, sir."

The rest of the week flew past, and Silas was busy enough with his own work, and with the occasional assist to Cyril, that he hardly had time to consider his evening with Ezra Curiel. It was only in odd moments, walking home from work or in bed late at night, that he thought about the boxer.

It was unusual for him to obsess about a particular man. Since his first experiences as a youth, he'd been happy to move from one cock to another with expediency, rarely lingering for more than a single encounter. He had seen what happened when he experienced romantic feelings, as he had with the man he'd been discovered with back home in Sheffield.

He'd been a fool, of course. The man was the father of a friend, married and under no circumstances could there have been a future between them. But then his father discovered the two of them together. His father had punched him in the face and disowned him. Fortunately his lover had arranged for him to clerk for a barrister in Birmingham, and so he'd been able to rebuild his life.

There was no way he was going to let any feelings for another man put him in such danger again. And yet, as Friday approached, he wondered if Ezra Curiel would be boxing again at New Cross. He convinced himself that it was not sentimentality to want to know what had happened between them the previous week.

He thought if he went back to the molly bar he'd find someone to distract him, but no one appealed to him. Finally he gave in and walked through the darkened streets of Rotherhithe toward the boxing arena.

The handbill posted on the wall promised that the Hammering Hebrew would fight in the third round of matches. Silas bought his ticket and walked inside. The high-ceilinged arena, which included boxing and wrestling rings, a weightlifting area and hanging punch bags, smelled of sweat and tobacco.

The second match was underway as he found himself a place to stand in the back. And while both men were well-built, and seemed to be competent boxers, neither of them appealed to him.

Would he feel anything when Ezra walked out? He'd have to wait and see.

The match ended and the ring was cleared up for the next pair of boxers. Ezra walked out to much acclaim, and Silas kept his head down. He didn't want to catch Ezra's eye for fear that Ezra might slip away without Silas catching him after the fight was over.

The match was long and drawn-out. Ezra's strength seemed to be in his footwork, his ability to dance away from punches, but when they landed, it was clear they hurt. He finally simply dove in and began hammering away at his opponent, living up to his name, and eventually he wore the other man down.

There was much rejoicing in the stands. Apparently many

people had bet on Ezra and were happy at his win. Silas hustled through the crowd and out to the street where he'd waited for Ezra before. He anxiously moved from foot to foot, partly because of the chill in the air, and partly because he was nervous. What if he'd made a fool of himself with Ezra, and deliberately blocked it out? What if Ezra had rejected him after all that wine?

There was only one way to find out. This time he'd brought a pen with him, and he waited until the crowd around Ezra cleared out to walk up to him. "Sign my program, Mr. Curiel?" he asked, as boldly as he could.

Ezra looked at him with a grin. He took the pen and scrawled, "For Silas, who can't hold his wine. Ezra Curiel."

Then he handed the program back to Silas, who read it open-mouthed.

"What happened?" he demanded.

Ezra looked around to make sure no one could overhear them. "I attempted to seduce you with wine, but you went overboard, and I had to push you into a carriage, and pay the driver to get you into your room." He looked at Silas. "Did he succeed?"

Finally Silas remembered. The carriage driver hauling him out, and standing beside him as he vomited in the street. The driver took his key from him and half-dragged him up to the front door. At Silas's direction, they'd climbed to his apartment, where the driver had unlocked the door and pushed him inside.

Then left.

"You could have seen me home yourself," he said.

Ezra shrugged. "Or I could have left you in the wine bar. You'd have woken up eventually. Probably when they tossed you out into the street." He paused. "But I am not that kind of man. Though I fight with my hands, I still consider myself a gentleman."

"We'll see how gentle you are when I get you back to my room," Silas said. "And this time no dilly-dallying about with wine."

Ezra laughed, and his mouth morphed into a ear-splitting grin. "You're a cheeky fellow, aren't you? I like that."

Chapter 4

Coquette

Ezra

Ezra hailed a carriage. "7 Bryanston Mews West," he said to the driver, and then climbed in.

Silas followed him. "You remembered my address."

Ezra nodded. "If you hadn't shown up tonight I thought of stopping by. Would I have found you there? Or would you have been out at a bar looking for a new companion?"

Silas crossed his arms over his chest. "I might have been."

"Ah, but you weren't," Ezra said. "You came to find me. To apologize, perhaps, for getting too drunk and falling asleep last week?"

"It was the wine!" Silas protested. "You wooed me with wine that was too strong for my delicate constitution."

"You look quite sturdy to me. But then I have not seen you without your clothes yet."

"And you still might not," Silas pouted, though it was all for show.

The carriage was closed, and there was no danger anyone could see them. Ezra leaned over and put his rough hand on Silas's jaw. Then, wary of the carriage's bumps, he drew Silas's face close to his and kissed him, so delicately that their lips barely touched.

Silas was clearly the type who moved fast and hard. He pressed his lips against Ezras's and pushed his tongue out. His left hand moved to Ezra's hip.

Ezra considered himself quite skilled at this kind of fight. He pulled back from the kiss, and lifted Silas's hand back to his own thigh. "All in good time," he said. "You have no other plans for the evening? No other lovers lined up?"

"You take me for a coquette," Silas said, pouting again.

Ezra's smile was broad. "And am I wrong?"

Silas waited a beat. "Well. No."

Ezra laughed. "I like you, Mr. Silas Warner. I believe we shall have fun together."

The carriage arrived, and Ezra paid the driver. He let Silas step out first, and then before he did so himself, he looked up and down the street. Only a few pedestrians out, all of them women. It was safe.

"This is now two fares I have paid to this address," he said to Silas as they mounted the steps to the front door. "I shall have some recompense, certainly?"

"As you wish," Silas said, and deliberately bumped his arse back against Ezra's crotch.

Ezra was startled, and pushed Silas forward to the security of the other side of the door. The man was a flirt, and clearly comfortable bringing other men home with him, and there might be someone watching through a window.

Once inside, he relaxed. They climbed the stairs quickly to Silas's room. "Welcome to my humble *maison*," Silas said, as he ushered Ezra inside, taking advantage of the chance to grope Ezra's buttocks.

"More like a *chambre* than a *maison*," Ezra said, looking around. The room was large enough to contain a double bed, a wardrobe, and a low table with a pitcher and basin. Colorful scarves hung from the ceiling and the bedposts, and pictures of scantily clad athletes had been posted on the walls.

"I see you have an eye for the male physique," Ezra said. He walked over to the wall to look more closely. "But I do not see a picture of me. Are these all your conquests?"

"Would that it were so," Silas said.

Ezra turned to see the man standing before him, completely naked. With all his costuming removed, he looked a bit pitiful. Not nearly as muscular as the men Ezra was accustomed to seeing in the dressing room at New Cross, with skinny arms and a faint trace of hair on his chest. His thighs were strong, though, and his cock was ample enough.

Ezra put his hands on his hips. "I hope you are not so quick at making love," he said.

"I can be fast, and I can be slow," Silas said. "Which do you prefer?"

"I prefer a man I can hold in my thrall for hours," Ezra said. Then he dropped to his knees, still fully clothed, and quickly took Silas's cock in his mouth.

"Oh!" Silas's voice was a mix of moan, surprise, and pleasure, and he continued to make such noises as Ezra sucked him.

When Ezra was still a lad, before he had developed his musculature, he learned to pleasure older boys in this way. It was when he first discovered that the Christian boys had not been cut around the top of their cocks, and they had a lovely extra flap of skin there to be teased and played with.

He performed that service to Silas, sucking him expertly until he sensed the Brit was about to spend, then pulling back and standing up. Silas went to grab his dick and finish the job, but Ezra took hold of his arm and pulled it away. "Who is in charge here?" he asked.

Silas's body seemed to melt. "You are."

"Indeed. You will take my jacket off, please. And hang it up so that it does not wrinkle."

"Yes, sir," Silas said.

"A simple yes will suffice," Ezra said, as Silas took the jacket off. "I am not your better, though perhaps a slight bit more than your equal."

He directed Silas through the removal of his shirt, his undershirt, his shoes, and his slacks. "This must be what having a valet is like," Ezra said. "Though I doubt most of the men of my acquaintance who have such servants require them to perform in the nude."

"I have heard of some," Silas said.

Ezra stood there and struck a boxing pose. "Tell me, which part of my anatomy do you prefer?"

"Do you mean of those currently on display?" Silas asked, as Ezra still wore his undershorts. His cock was already quite stiff and pressing against the thin fabric.

"Yes. Please show me."

Silas began with his biceps, which were strong and wiry, and if he were to be honest, Ezra's greatest pride. Yes, his body was muscular and his cock was sufficient, but he loved to appraise his own arms and feel the strength in them.

"These arms are so strong in the fight, but I wonder if they can be gentle as well," Silas said. "I would like to be held by them."

"And so you shall be." Ezra brought Silas close to him, Silas's back to his front, and reached around to hold the skinny man. His hands folded together over Silas's breastbone in a manner that was quite pleasing. Then he leaned down and licked behind Silas's ear, and set him shivering with delight.

"Your hands," Silas said. "They are a man's hands, rough and bruised, yet I see you wear gloves at the arena. Don't those gloves protect your hands?"

"I boxed for many years without gloves," Ezra said. "And sometimes I forego them in practice rounds. There is nothing like the feel of skin against skin, is there?"

Silas responded by pressing his naked arse against Ezra's groin. Ezra unloosed his hands and they roamed down Silas's flat belly, stopping just above the thatch of dark blond hair that surrounded his cock.

Silas twisted around so that he faced Ezra, and once again folded himself into Ezra's grasp. But now they were face to face, and could continue the kissing they had begun in the cab, accompanied by the occasional nipple twist or press of their groins together.

By then Ezra's cock was weeping into his shorts, and he discarded them. As soon as his cock was free, Silas attacked it with fervor, licking and sucking. Ezra appreciated his enthusiasm as much as his technique, which involved a finger beneath his bollocks that was designed to drive him insane.

Though he wanted to hold back, he couldn't, and he spent in Silas's mouth.

They fell to the bed together, and it seemed to Ezra like each of them was determined to outdo the other in creative approaches to sex. When Silas had spent, and then Ezra had spent again, this time in Silas's surprisingly sweet arse, they collapsed together and Silas moved close, resting his head on Ezra's chest.

"How did you know that is my favorite position?" Ezra said. Too often the men he had been with had been eager to spend and then move on, while Ezra thought the best part of sex was the afterglow, the feeling of another man in his arms.

"Because it is mine," Silas said. "You see all those handsome men on the walls? Yes, I would like to suck them and have them fuck me. But most of all I would like to be held for a moment or two."

Ezra leaned down and kissed Silas's tousled hair. "I can manage that," he said.

They dozed like that for several hours, until Ezra woke to relieve himself. He used the toilet in the hall and then returned to Silas's room. He slept like an angel, with a smile on his face.

Ezra knew that he could dress then, and sneak out, and leave it up to Silas to chase after him, if he wanted. Or he could slip back under the sheets beside Silas, and wake again with him in the morning light.

Chapter 5

The Sweet Science

Silas

Silas usually tried to stand at the front whenever he watched Ezra fight, but that night, a Saturday evening in November 1875, he had arrived late at the ring in New Cross. He had to fight for a place, wedged in among smoking, cheering, bowler-hat-wearing men.

Around him, men bet on the outcome of the six-round spars and the main event. The man next to him drank deeply from a hip flask then asked, "Who d'you figure for the last spar?"

That was an easy answer. "My money's on Curiel," Silas said. "He hasn't lost a bout in the last three weeks."

"I bet on him often," the man said, smiling. "I consider him my lucky talisman. Unfortunately he has gained such a reputation that the odds always seem to favor him, and there is little money to be made when he wins."

"He's in fine form this week," Silas said. "I saw him practicing yesterday. He's getting his sleep, eating well. I wouldn't waste money on a bet against him."

The man turned to look at Silas. He was a dark-haired fellow a bit shorter than Silas himself, and Silas was no giant. "You know him well, then?"

Silas shrugged. "I'm a follower." There was no way he could tell this stranger how close his relationship with Ezra was, how it had developed over the last few weeks.

"Nathan Walpert," the man said, sticking out his hand.

"Silas Warner. I've seen you here before. You follow any other boxer in particular?"

"Whoever I think I can make a few quid on." Nathan waved over the boy who took bets for Benny Greenbaum, one of the most notorious of the London bookmakers. "I'll take your advice," he said to Silas. He handed a bill to the boy. "Put this on the Hammering Hebrew."

The boy scribbled out a chit and handed it to Nathan, then followed the hail of another man.

Most of the boxers in the early spars practiced what Silas had learned was called "catch as catch can," which meant a combination of Irish, Scottish, and other regional styles of boxing, including jabs, footwork, and wrestling moves. Though he'd been drawn originally purely to see muscular, sweaty men grappling with each other, Ezra had begun training Silas to recognize specific moves and their effect on the eventual outcome of the fight.

"What about you?" Nathan asked. "You don't bet?"

Silas shook his head. "My pocketbook is too empty to risk anything. I just like watching the men."

Something in Nathan's eyes said he did the same, despite his talk about betting. He offered Silas a swig from his flask, and Silas took it, relishing the taste the man's lips had left on it. He would have said something risqué—but he was meeting Ezra after the match and saving his spend to spurt over the boxer later that evening.

It was unusual for him, he had to admit, that he had fixed on one man for so long. But there was something about Ezra's muscular physique and his thick, fat cock that kept Silas coming back for more. And each new man he met could not compare.

Silas was grateful for the use of gloves in the ring, as he savored the touch of Ezra's hands, which were already bruised and calloused after years of bare-knuckle sparring. He was also worried about Ezra's future—fighters who survived past forty had limited opportunities ahead of them. Ezra knew many stories of fighters who turned to training or used their strength in back-breaking labors. Still others had become hired muscle for criminal operations.

Though Ezra had gained some renown and was often the subject of much betting, he was relegated to the last of the spars. That placement gave his many fans, and an equal number of detractors, the opportunity to enter many bets for and against him.

Silas waited through the first five rounds, suffering to watch boxers who could not match Ezra's physique or technique, though he did find himself hardening when one fighter's shorts accidentally slipped below his waist, exposing a fair bit of cheek and the top of his arse crack.

"Will you bet on the final match?" Silas asked Nathan. "After Curiel?"

It was to bring together a black African fighter who had not lost a fight in two years and a hulking pugilist recently released from a spell in prison, after punching not only his female romantic interest but a pair of bobbies who tried to arrest him as well.

"If my bet on my fellow comes through," Nathan said.

Silas was surprised. Why would this bettor in his business suit call Ezra 'my fellow.' Had he been partaking of Ezra's cock as Silas had?

"I call him a fellow only because I've seen him at synagogue once or twice," Nathan said. He hesitated and then added, "A fellow Jew."

They were still preparing the ring, and Nathan's whiskey had gone to his head a bit, so Silas dared ask, "Is it true that all Jews have had their cocks cut off at the tip?"

"It is a tradition among our people," Nathan said. "At eight days after birth. Said to reduce the chance of sickness."

Nathan took another swig of his whiskey, and Silas felt his cock hardening as he watched the man's lips form an O around the spout of the flask. "I take it you haven't been – cut," Nathan said.

"I haven't."

"Does it make a difference?" Nathan asked. "Most of the fellows I know are in the same situation I am, and I've never known a chap outside my religion I could ask."

Silas didn't know what to say. Until meeting Ezra, and discovering the difference in his cock, he'd never heard of the rite called circumcision. All the other cocks he'd sucked had come with foreskin. He did notice that his own was particularly sensitive, particularly on the rare occasions when he penetrated another man.

But how much to reveal to this stranger. "From what I've heard it's an extra bit of pleasure," he finally said. "To the man. I can't speak for the woman's part."

He was relieved when Ezra walked out, his hands raised and his fists clenched, and he and Nathan both turned their attention to the ring. Silas cheered himself hoarse at the sight of Ezra, shirtless in yellow knee-length pantaloons and white socks that reached up to meet them. His opponent, Lawrence Fulham, was barely out of his teens, a hefty bull of a fellow in similar attire. It appeared to Silas that he was more fleshy than muscular.

The bell rang and they faced each other. As he had learned from his compatriot Daniel Mendoza, another Sephardic Jew who had boxed in those rings a few decades earlier, Ezra fought with his knees bent and his arms guarding his face.

He danced around Fullham, landing a few punches to the bigger man's face. It quickly became clear that while Fullham's hands packed a powerful wallop, he was slow on his feet. Within the first minutes, Ezra knocked his opponent to the ground, and a moment after he rose to his feet, the younger man suddenly fainted.

"Swooning like a lady," one man called, and others took up the chant with "Lady Man! Lady Man!"

Silas shivered to think how they would react to know that they had a real 'lady-man' in the audience among them. It frightened him.

The men booed and money began to change hands. Nathan clapped Silas on the shoulder. "The odds weren't great, but I won," he crowed. "For a change!"

Silas congratulated him and then fought his way through the crowd to the exit. He turned the corner and lingered in the dark alley outside the boxing ring.

He wondered how Nathan would have reacted if Silas had suggested a quick suck in that alley while he waited for Ezra. He remembered how Nathan's mouth had formed that sweet O while drinking his whiskey and wondered if the man would have been willing to suck him.

Probably not, he thought. Nathan had been wearing a gold ring, which meant he was married, and he would have expected Silas to do what his wife wouldn't.

Not that he would have minded. It might have been fun to suck another Jewish cock to compare to Ezra's. But Ezra was strong and jealous, and it wouldn't do to get caught by him. Not that Ezra had ever hurt him—he reserved his anger for those who oppressed him because of his religion, or who blocked his further ascent in the boxing world. He relished the use of his body in all areas, including fucking. It was a marvel to watch the muscles and tendons in his arms and legs move as he posed for Silas, or thrust himself into Silas's arse.

He came out of the back door a few minutes later, while Silas was still fully aroused by the thought of sucking Nathan's cock. Seeing no one around, he pressed himself against Ezra. "I love watching you move about the ring," he said, desperate to shift his brain away from Ezra's fellow Hebrew.

"And you will see me move even more when I take you to bed," Ezra said. He grabbed Silas by the waist and pressed their bodies together, and Silas worried that he might spend right there. But then Ezra pushed him back and laughed.

"Fullham clearly hasn't mastered the sweet science," Silas said. It was a term he'd learned from Ezra, originally coined by a journalist to describe the use of tactics and strategies to win a match.

"He's young. He'll learn," Ezra said. "Though I had a fright when he fainted. Worried I'd damaged something inside."

"Well, he got up, and he'll live to fight another day," Silas said.

The air was particularly fetid that night, and after spending so much time in the smoky arena Silas began to cough. Wary of attracting attention, Ezra hailed a carriage to take them to Silas's rooms.

"You spoil me, you know," Silas said, as they got out of the carriage.

"And I intend to spoil you even further when we reach your bed." Ezra gave Silas's buttocks a slap, and Silas jerked forward an inch and felt his cock begin to unfurl in his pants.

Once again, Ezra surveyed the street before leaving the carriage. He knew the dangers of being caught with a man like Silas, but something pushed him forward.

They hurried upstairs. "I save up my energy before a fight, as you know," Ezra said, once inside the door. He began stripping his clothes quickly. "And because Fullham went down so quickly, I have all that energy bursting to get out."

Silas was quick to shuck his clothes, tossing them over a nearby chair, so that when he and Ezra faced each other, both were naked. "I shall never tire of seeing your body revealed to me," Silas said. "You are the most perfect Adonis."

Ezra's body was not perfect to most eyes. The knuckles on his right hand were red and scraped from his bare-knuckle practice that afternoon. He had a long scar like a snake on the right side of his chest, and other smaller ones on his arms and legs. He held his right arm at a slight angle, the result of tendon injuries. But in Silas's eyes his bulging muscles and his meaty cock made up for all that.

"And as Adonis was a Greek god, you should worship me as a French one," Ezra said, planting his feet on the carpet and putting his hands on his hips. His erect cock stood out from his body like a slanted flagpole, the foreskin noticeably absent.

Silas needed no further direction. He dropped to his knees and put his right hand beneath Ezra's bollocks, positioning the man's cock for entry into his mouth. He swallowed it whole, and Ezra groaned.

"Such velvet," he said.

As he knew Ezra liked, Silas squeezed the man's bollocks as he sucked, coaxing the spend to rise. "Oh, my pretty, pretty boy," Ezra said. He dipped his fingers into Silas's blond curls and massaged his skull.

Both of them were so worked up that Ezra spent very quickly, and Silas swallowed all but a few drops, which dribbled from his lips. He stood, his cock stiff, and they kissed deeply.

"I love to taste myself on your tongue," Ezra said. He grabbed Silas by the buttocks and pressed him forward, so that Silas's cock was up against his lover's skin.

Ezra began a slow, sensuous dance, and his sweat and the clear fluid that came out of Silas's cock lubricated them, skin on skin, as they frotted. Ezra was so strong he had Silas off his feet, those muscular hands gripping Silas's buttocks, as they swayed together, faster and faster until Silas felt his blood rise. He gasped for breath as the orgasm overtook him and he spilled against Ezra's groin.

Ezra did not release his grip until Silas's orgasm had subsided and he could breathe normally. Then he set Silas down carefully. "My feet have nearly fallen asleep," Silas said. He leaned against Ezra and shook one leg out, and then the other. "A small price to pay for such a great pleasure."

"And more to come," Ezra said. "I have been saving my loads for you." He laughed. "It is not as if Rebecca wants them, or I want to give them to her."

Silas ignored the reference to Ezra's wife, as he preferred to do. He wet a washcloth from the ewer on the bureau and cleaned them both up, and then they reclined together on the bed, under the canopy of colorful scarves that brightened the otherwise dark and dismal room.

"How has your work been this week?" Ezra asked.

"As I have said, one must have a wide range of skills to be a barrister's clerk, and I have been improving those since my first position in Birmingham, where I did little more than run errands and copy documents. But I observed everything that went on around me and made myself useful."

"As you have been useful for me," Ezra said.

"Though in a different realm," Silas said. He reached over and pinched Ezra's right nipple, which he knew his lover fancied. "I aspire to becoming Barrister Pemberton's senior clerk someday. That position requires commercial acumen, legal knowledge, and strong communication skills."

He turned on his side. "Cyril Alderton is responsible for negotiating rates, attending client meetings, and forging relationships with solicitors, who are in a position to refer their criminal cases."

"And this Mr. Alderton. He is an elderly fellow, soon to depart this mortal coil?"

Silas shook his head. "No, he is barely in his forties, so unless he finds a better position I will be a junior clerk for quite some time. He has, however, been sickly of late, leading to worry on Pemberton's part."

They chatted for a while, back and forth about boxing and the law and the affairs of the day, until Ezra began running his index finger along Silas's chest, tickling through the scant blond hairs there.

"Ding, ding," Silas said, imitating the bell at the boxing ring. "Ready for the next match?"

With quick agility, Ezra hopped over so that he was straddling Silas. He grabbed Silas's hands with his own and stretched them up toward the bedposts. "Stay like that, mon cher," he said.

He jumped off the bed and walked over to Silas's bureau, where he extracted a pair of blue and green paisley scarves from the bottom drawer, along with a bottle of oil. He quickly tied Silas's wrists to the bedpost. Then he lifted Silas's legs and scooted under them, resting Silas's calves on his broad shoulders.

He sat on his knees and used his right fist to oil his cock, which by then had come back to full stature. Using the fingers of that same hand, he began lubricating Silas's arsehole, with first one finger, then two, then three, until it relaxed and opened like a blossom in spring.

He scooted up close to Silas and positioned his cock at the entrance, and began to gently push his way in. "More," Silas panted. "I want all of you inside me."

"My pleasure, mon cher," Ezra said, and began to use his powerful hips to thrust farther and farther into Silas, until Silas felt that this was the way he always wanted to be, holding close to the most delicate part of his lover, feeling his insides expanding to envelop him.

Ezra's earlier need to spend had been taken care of, so now he was slow and strong and persistent. Sweat dripped from his forehead and from beneath his arms as he held his position and moved in and out, determined to make this last. And last it did, until after Silas had spontaneously spent, accompanied by high-pitched whines and animal noises. Silas looked deep into his lover's eyes then, and could almost pinpoint the moment when Ezra's orgasm overcame him, and he spilled into Silas's chute.

The journalist Pierce Egan may have called boxing the sweet science, Silas thought then. But lovemaking was surely as sweet.

Chapter 6

The Boxer

Raoul

"I cannot wait to introduce you to my latest lover," Silas said. He collapsed on the divan in the living room of the rooms his friend Raoul Desjardins shared with his lover, John Seales, Lord Therkenwell.

"I don't know which hurts worse," Silas continued. "My heart or my bollocks, which can only be emptied by Ezra Curiel. I have not been able to see him all week, because he traveled to Liverpool for a series of weekday matches. At least he will be at New Cross this evening, and I will see him afterward."

"Curiel?" Raoul asked. "The boxer?"

"Indeed. He is a most masterful man, in the ring and in the boudoir."

Raoul poured glasses of wine for both of them, then sat across from Silas. "How in the world did you come in contact with him?"

"I have taken to attending boxing matches." Silas sipped the wine and smiled. He had developed more of a taste and tolerance for wine since meeting Ezra. "The fighters are so muscular, and with their shirts off everything is on display. Their bodies are oiled, and when they tense up, or swing their fists, you can see every tendon and sinew." He sighed extravagantly. "It is so much more erotic than spying on men at the seaside."

"And Curiel has a body you admire?"

"Oh, my Lord. He is swarthy, you know, which is an extra bit for me. I have had always a taste for darker meat. He is a Spanish Jew, by way of Algeria and France, and so his skin is naturally more colored than mine, or even yours."

Raoul's skin was darker than Silas's, which was so fair it could light up the night, though Raoul did not think himself particularly swarthy. He had to admit that his jet-black hair to Silas's blond, and the hair that covered his arms, chest and legs, did tend to darken his overall appearance.

"How did you encounter him? At a molly house?"

Silas shook his head. "No, at one of his fights. I was in the front, and I caught his eye and smiled, and he smiled back." He leaned back in a swoon. "And so it began!"

"You did not stalk him, did you?" Raoul was aware of Silas's hyperactive temperament, and he could see his friend following the boxer around London observing him and waiting for a moment to approach him.

"Indeed I did not," Silas protested. "I will admit, I waited around in the alley outside the boxing hall until after all the cards had been finished. Ezra's eyes positively lit up when he saw me standing there. It was as if someone had struck a match, igniting our two candles at once."

Silas reached down to grab his cock, to make the metaphor complete, and Raoul laughed.

"And did he take you right there in the alley?"

Silas crossed his arms over his chest, affronted. "I am not that much of an easy mark," he said. "He offered to buy me a glass of wine first."

Raoul laughed. "And then?"

"Then it was like one of those fairy tales by your Monsieur Perrault. We spoke, we touched hands, we fell headlong into love."

"Or lust."

"Well, lust at first, certainly. Unfortunately I do not have a Frenchman's tolerance for wine, so I fell asleep before he could bed me. He was such a gentleman, though. He paid a carriage driver to take me home and tuck me in."

"So you bedded the carriage driver instead."

Silas shook his head. "I was so drunk I might have, but there was no evidence the next morning. I had to wait until the following Friday to return to the boxing arena and try once more. Fortunately I was able to draw him to my petite apartment, where he ravished me so completely that I could barely remember my own name."

Raoul smiled. John had the ability to ravish him in the very same way. He poured another round of wine into the globe-shaped glasses. He marveled yet again at the luxury which he enjoyed now that John had invited him to share his rooms at Eaton Square in the Bloomsbury section of London. Surely, love was wonderful.

Silas drank deeply. "Since then, we have become a regular item. I attend his boxing matches, and he comes home with me afterwards."

"And his wife does not notice, or does not care?"

"Theirs was a marriage of convenience," Silas said, waving his hand in the air. "Her father is a wealthy Parisian merchant, but because she has a sharp tongue she could not find a husband. Ezra showed no intention of marrying, focusing on his body and his developing career as a boxer."

He sipped his wine again. "He and Ezra's father were compatriots of the same Parisian synagogue, and both wished their children to be married. Madame Curiel's father settled a sizeable amount on the new couple, which allowed them to escape their fathers' thumbs and come to England."

He finished his glass and held it out to Raoul for a refill. "He is unhappy but does not know how he can escape the marriage now."

"So he is forced to seek solace in your boudoir," Raoul said.

"I hardly have to force him," Silas said. "If anything, he is the one who exerts the force. He enjoys tying my arms and legs to the bedpost and attacking my arse with his tongue, until I am as loose as a plate of sizzling oil and begging him to spear me with his sausage."

Raoul held up his hand. "Please, spare me the details. How long has this been going on?"

"We shall celebrate the three-month anniversary of our meeting next week," Silas said. He laughed. "I know, you will chide me for such sentimentality, which I have never before felt, and in the past derided. But I cannot help myself."

It made Raoul happy to see his friend's enjoyment, but he worried about what might happen if the boxer was to be reeled back in by his wife, and forced to forswear male company. He had seen it happen in Paris, and once or twice in London as well.

He and John had been helped out of a tricky situation by the mentorship of a more established couple, Lord Magnus Dawson and his lover, Toby Marsh. Since then, they had been brought into a social circle that opened their eyes to the wide array of entanglements men who loved men often found themselves in.

There were older men with younger lovers, and men who were married to women but sought occasional pleasure in the arms of other men. He had met those who could only express their desires in secret or with anonymous encounters. And those who for reasons of family wealth or social pressure could not be open.

He sat back with his wine in his hand and his legs spread. He knew of men of the lower classes who sometimes had more freedom than their betters. The tavern he and John frequented was owned by a pair of men, one of whom dressed as a woman to serve customers, and no one batted an eye.

Of course, half the patrons had no idea what was under the barmaid's skirts, so clever was her disguise.

Too often, though, he had seen affairs like the one between Silas and Ezra come apart, and suffered the wails and torrents of tears that accompanied such a break. He only hoped that Silas would be the exception, though it was hard to see such a public figure and avatar of masculinity as Ezra Curiel squiring the flamboyant Silas Warner around town in his Indonesian silk robes and colorful peacock shirts.

Silas could have his quiet side, however. He dressed very plainly at work and kept his flamboyance in check there.

"Well, I hope you shall both be very happy," Raoul said, though he could not see a way forward to such an event. He and John narrowly escaped the prejudices that accompanied male unions by virtue of John's title and his family wealth. The same was the case for Magnus and Toby, and for their female friends the Honorable Sylvia Cooke and her companion Miss Cleaver. And Ezra Curiel had already cultivated too large a public persona to disappear into anonymity as the bar owners had.

Raoul quieted a sigh. Silas would do as he would, and Raoul and John would be there to pick up the pieces as necessary.

Chapter 7

Sylvia's Party

Silas

Silas had been invited to join John and Raoul at a dinner party on Saturday night, and since Ezra was out of town for a series of fights, he had eagerly accepted. He arrived at their apartment on Russell Square in Bloomsbury.

"Where is your lover tonight?" Raoul asked Silas.

"Newcastle," Silas said. "It is his first chance to be in the featured fight. One last night and one tonight, and he returns to London tomorrow afternoon." He relaxed on the divan in John and Raoul's apartment. "Tell me again the reason for this party."

"It is to celebrate the thirtieth birthday of the Honorable Sylvia Cooke," John said. "She is a childhood friend of Magnus."

"Will it be stuffy, with all lots of titled people?"

"Not at all," John said. "Sylvia and Jess are hosting a tea this afternoon to which Sylvia's posh connections will be invited. Then when they are gone, we will join them for dinner and dancing afterward, in what I expect will be very louche company."

"Magnus and Toby have sent their houseboy and cook to help prepare the food and the decorations," Raoul said.

Then they walked to the home the Sylvia and Jess occupied in a narrow house in a mews directly off Jermyn Street. It had the advantage of a prestigious address, yet was compact and perfect for an unmarried woman of the gentry and her companion. They had a housemaid and a cook. Because Jenny and Marian were a Sapphic couple as well, no one ever mentioned that Sylvia and Jess shared the same bed.

The three of them ran into Magnus and Toby on Jermyn Street.

It was easy to discern Toby Marsh's hand in Magnus Dawson attire. His cravat was tied to perfection and he wore an elegant waistcoat, suit jacket, and knee-length topcoat.

Magnus's waistcoat was black with a collar of maroon velvet. Toby's was of a similar color but without a contrasting collar. They had matching top hats—purchased at the same time from the same vendor. They never knew which belonged to each, and wore them interchangeably.

The door was opened by a tall woman of athletic bearing, in a long dress in pale pink satin with a voluminous skirt. It perfectly complemented her English-rose complexion.

"I hardly recognize you out of your normal attire of trousers under a nipped waistcoat," Magnus said. "I hate to celebrate your birthday, my dear, because it means that mine will soon follow," Magnus said, as he kissed Sylvia's cheek.

"And yet when we were children we were so eager for our birthdays to occur," Sylvia said.

"You look particularly fetching today," Toby said, as he kissed Sylvia's cheek. "One could easily assume you were just past your debut."

"Oh, that awful year," Sylvia said. "Do you recall, Magnus? You were my constant attendant at all those parties. We must have danced our feet off."

"We did indeed. You know John and Raoul, of course. And this is their friend Silas, who is a barrister's clerk at the Inns of Court."

"Happy birthday," Silas said, as he leaned down to kiss Sylvia's outstretched hand.

"Lovely manners," Sylvia said. "You may keep him." She turned to all of them. "May we offer you a cocktail? Will is engaged, but I know Magnus can find his way around a bar."

"Indeed," Magnus said. "There is champagne, sugar and water to hand, as well as some sliced fruit left over from the tea garnish. Shall I make a round of champagne cobblers?"

"That would be delightful," Sylvia said.

Magnus led the way to the bar at the side of the sitting room. The wing chairs had been upholstered in a satin fabric of Chinese look, with colorful birds and flowers. Soft, natural light filtered through the large windows that faced the mews, creating a warm and inviting atmosphere.

"How was your tea party earlier?" Magnus asked.

Jess joined them from the kitchen, where she had been supervising the preparation of the hors d'oeuvres. She had a long face that was emphasized by her straight blonde hair, which hung like a curtain over either ear. Her dress was a dark green velour with a full skirt and a white lace collar. She kissed the cheeks of the gentlemen.

"The tea party went off without a hitch," Jess said. "We had a string quartet, and a lovely table of petits fours and other desserts. We must have had twenty women in all, mostly those of London society."

She turned to Sylvia. "You must tell them about your newest acquaintance, the chair of the Soup Kitchen for the Jewish Poor at Spitalfields."

"Yes, Mrs. Rebecca Curiel," Sylvia said. "I have had occasion to attend some of her charity fund-raisers and thought it appropriate to invite her here, so she could recruit other donors."

"Mrs. Curiel?" Silas asked in astonishment. "Is her husband by chance a boxer?"

Sylvia looked at him. "I am not surprised you recognize the name. He is known as the Hammering Hebrew, and Magnus has mentioned attending his fights."

"I have been on occasion, though I would not call myself a devotee," he said. He turned to Silas. "Are you a fan of his?"

Raoul and John began to laugh, and everyone turned to them, as Silas's pale face reddened.

"Silas is a bit more than a fan," John said, when he was able to stop laughing. "He is the boxer's lover."

"That explains a great deal," Sylvia said. "I mentioned that Magnus has been known to attend the fights, and that I might suggest he look for her husband. She said that she could not advise Magnus to bet on him, as of late he has been quite distracted at home, and she worried that will carry over to the boxing ring."

Silas was still too embarrassed to say anything.

"According to his wife, he has no other talent beyond his fists, you see, and she fears what will happen to him when his career is ended," Jess said. "It was unusual for a woman to speak so frankly about her husband, though perhaps Mrs. Curiel's unfamiliarity with high society led her to be open. Or she considered me somewhere between the ladies and the help and could more easily confide in me."

"I was delighted when the last of the ladies left," Sylvia said. "I thought they would never go," she said.

"If you didn't want a party, why have one?" Toby asked.

"I owed many social obligations, and this seemed a useful way to pay them back. And I was able to arrange some introductions between wealthy donors and charity volunteers. Mrs. Curiel secured contributions from several of my more moneyed acquaintances. So it served its purpose."

"We all must have a purpose," Raoul said. "Of course you know of John's broadsides. I know that he is champing at the bit to ask you about his latest project."

"I do not appreciate being compared to a horse, my love," John said. "But your infelicitous comment does allow me to raise my question. I have been chasing down a story for my next broadside. What do any of you know of this deal for Britain to purchase shares in the Suez Canal?"

"Just that the deal cannot go through until Parliament returns in session," Magnus said. "Prime Minister Disraeli does not have the personal funds to advance her majesty's government the four million pounds necessary."

"Ah, but his friend Lionel de Rothschild does," John said. "There are rumors that he will provide Disraeli a loan until the government can convene to approve the expenditure."

"And what does Janner think of that?" Toby asked.

Janner was the nom de plume that John used when publishing his broadsides. He'd adopted the name because it meant an English person born within ten miles of the sea, and he thought it suited him, as he was a Cornishman through and through, connected to the peninsula where he had been born and raised. It also served a shield between his noble title and his rabble-rousing work.

"Janner does not believe the government should take any action without proper debate," John said. "What if this deal turns bad? Who will be at risk? Her majesty's government cannot be called to account for a deal it has not approved."

"Then it will be between Mr. Disraeli and Mr. Rothschild, won't it?" Raoul asked. The year before, after a scandal involving his boss, Raoul had ascended to that man's position, as undersecretary for British affairs at the French embassy. "Wouldn't that be interesting, if one of London's biggest banks went into partnership with my government, which Britain still regards as a potential enemy."

"What is the official French position about giving up partial control of the Canal to a British consortium?" Magnus asked Raoul as he sipped his champagne cocktail.

Raoul shrugged. "We would rather that control of the canal remain completely within French hands, for the purposes of security. However we are not opposed to the sale of shares to Britain because it will bring better political stability to the region."

Silas didn't have much of an opinion on politics or financial deals, but he enjoyed the company of his friends. It was much better than sitting at home alone and missing Ezra.

Ezra was providing him a source of both joy and consternation. He had never felt so deeply for a man before and he worried about that. He did not think himself a candidate for the kind of settled domesticity that his friends enjoyed. In the past, he'd been eager to taste the next cock, and easily bored by the same.

But there was something different about his feelings for Ezra, and that worried him. The man was a public figure, first. If he were revealed to be a sodomite, he'd surely lose his boxing career, and the consequent income. He was devoted to his religion, which Silas knew little about, but he assumed it was not welcoming toward men who loved men.

He had also noted the way that Ezra worried when they were in public, afraid that someone might recognize him and understand his inclinations. Magnus and Toby, and Raoul and John, had no such problems. None of them were public figures, and they were insulated by the titles that Magnus and John held.

The biggest obstacle, of course, was the marriage between Ezra and Rebecca. Silas could not imagine moving into the home they shared. They would be doomed to casual meetings for sex, which should have been enough, but clearly was not.

He was impressed when they entered the ladies' dining room. The dining table was the centerpiece of the room and was meticulously set with dinner plates, soup bowls, and dessert plates, all arranged with precision.

It was the first time Silas had ever been invited to such an elegant dinner, and he struggled to fight his feelings of insecurity. Despite his friendship with these higher-class men, he was still a laborer's son from Sheffield.

He marveled at the crystal glassware, including wine glasses, water goblets, and champagne flutes, glistened in the candlelight. Polished silverware, including forks, knives, and spoons, were placed in order beside the plates. The table was adorned with the fresh flower arrangements and candles flickered, casting a warm glow over the room.

He made sure to sit beside Raoul so he could copy his friend's attention to the meal, and hopefully avoid any faux pas.

"Toby and Magnus's cook Carlo has worked with ours to create an Italian-themed menu, to celebrate a visit Sylvia and I made to Italy last summer," Jess said as they sat. "The first course is a stracciatella, a soup that combines shredded chicken, spinach, basil, peas, grated Parmigiano-Reggiano, and eggs. Sylvia and I first tasted it in Portofino, and it reminds us of that lovely sun-drenched city."

Silas could not imagine having the means and the time to make such a trip. He hadn't left London since he had arrived.

"I found it interesting that you invited Mrs. Curiel to your tea this afternoon," Magnus said to Sylvia as they sipped the soup.

"Because of her religion?" Sylvia asked.

"Well, that, first," Magnus said. "The Jews tend to keep to themselves, don't they? Unless they are like Disraeli and have converted to the Anglican faith. I am familiar with a wine merchant by the name of Samuel Steingrob, and while we have knowledgeable discussions about wine I would never think to invite him to share my table. Nor would he expect that, given the dietary restrictions his people follow."

Magnus surveyed the table. "And I am surprised that you invited a boxer's wife, as well. I have seen some boxers engaged in their fights, and I would never expect to see one in my home."

"Because you are a prig, Magnus dear," Sylvia said, and the group laughed. "Just because a man works with his hands is no reason to exclude him, or his wife."

"But surely there are different classes of men who work with their hands," Magnus said. "We have had the man who makes our hats to dinner, and we have had excellent conversation."

"But a hatmaker you would employ surely works with the elite, and is comfortable chatting while measuring your cranium. Would you invite a bricklayer? A blacksmith?" Sylvia asked, as Will appeared to take away the soup bowls. Carlo was right behind him with a serving platter of spaghetti Bolognese, which he served to each guest.

At least Silas recognized that dish. "I am but a clerk," he said. "And you tolerate me at your home."

"There is no but about it," Magnus said. "You are charming and well-spoken, and you educate yourself constantly about the law. I should not be surprised to see you move to up to the position of senior clerk with a barrister any time. And I would be happy to speak with any man if he had something to say," Magnus said.

"If you would take the time to speak to a bricklayer, or a blacksmith, you might be surprised," John said. "I regularly speak with men on the street of all occupations and backgrounds. Some, admittedly, are common louts, but others are surprisingly well-spoken, though they have not had the advantages of education as you and I have."

"I had little formal education past the eighth grade," Jess said. "That's when I was sent to a cousin's to become a nanny. I spent my next six years in the company of children rather than my peers, so my education was stunted. Is that very different from a tradesman who left school at the same age?"

Silas felt comforted to know that he and Jess shared a similar background.

"I can see I am falling into a trap," Magnus said. "And so I shall withdraw my comment. John, if you would allow it, I should like to accompany you sometime to see the kinds of people you associate with, and perhaps learn to adjust my attitude."

"You are quite welcome to join me," John said. "On Monday, I will be visiting some of the properties my father owns in the East End to see how the tenants feel about being displaced, with the potential of relocation to better housing."

"How would you do that?" Lady Sylvia asked. "Surely the tenants must vacate their property for it to be demolished and then rebuilt. Where would they live in the interim?"

"That would be a matter for the developer," John said. "The American philanthropist George Peabody has set up a donation fund to assist with the development of properties and the relocation of those who are displaced."

They had finished their spaghetti, and once those plates were cleared Will brought out servings of roast rabbit accompanied by winter vegetables. "Carlo calls this course the secondi," he said, giving the last word an awkward attempt at Italian pronunciation.

The food smelled delicious, and everyone began to eat. "It is important that those of us who have been blessed with wealth and education should show some leadership," John said. "There are many laws in this nation which deserve adjustment, not the least those that face us because of our sexual situations."

"As everyone in this room should," Toby said. "Magnus and I face very different penalties, should we be arrested for the act of loving each other. As a lord, he might pay a fine, while I should be sentenced to hard labor."

There was a collective shudder in the room. Silas saw himself in that comment. He was from a poor background, though his connection with Richard Pemberton gave him a small bit of status. And Ezra, despite his reputation and the money he earned, was an immigrant and a Jew. He would have no one to protect him.

"Enough of such stuff," Sylvia said. "It is my birthday, and I command that we speak only of happy ideas. Jess and I were fortunate enough to see many great sights during our tour of Italy. The architecture, the art, the scenery. And of course the food, which Carlo has so deliciously imitated for us."

Carlo was brought out to accept applause from the diners, and he announced that he had prepared a special dessert for them, a tiramisu. "It is a creamy dessert of espresso-soaked ladyfingers surrounded by lightly sweetened whipped cream and a rich mascarpone," he said. "I hope you will like it."

"I am sure we will," Sylvia said.

They retired to the lounge after dinner to await the arrival of additional guests. During that time Will and the ladies' maid cleared the dining room and prepared it for dancing.

The tone of the party changed considerably as the new guests arrived, many of them male couples, or those in which one man assumed the attire of a female. There was much commentary over attire and makeup.

The quartet struck up a tune, and couples assembled for dancing. Though Magnus danced one round with Sylvia, as a birthday courtesy, Silas noted he seemed happiest to partner with Toby, who fit quite well in his arms. He regretted not having Ezra by his side, and wondered if the grace with which he boxed lent itself to dancing as well. He spent some good time fantasizing about what it would be like to twirl around the room with his lover.

All in all, he thought, it had been quite an enjoyable time. But he still waited eagerly for Ezra to return from Newcastle.

Chapter 8

Gallantee

Ezra

When Ezra returned from Newcastle Sunday afternoon it was a surprisingly fine day, with winds pushing the sooty air off toward the Channel, allowing the sun to shine. He stopped at his home to drop his case, expecting Rebecca to be out at one of her charity events, but she was in the sitting room composing a letter.

She was a fine-looking woman, he thought, her dark hair and eyes a contrast to her pale skin. It was a shame that he didn't love her, and even more of a shame that she tolerated it.

"Good afternoon," he said, and she looked up from her writing.

"How was Newcastle?"

"The Hammering Hebrew was a success. I won all three bouts."

"That's good. Were you hurt at all?"

He twisted his right wrist. "A few aches and pains. Nothing serious."

She sat back in her chair. "Have you considered what you will do when you can no longer box?"

"It would be tempting fate to do so. And besides, the Torah says

'The righteous cry, and the Lord hears and delivers them out of all their troubles.' If I can no longer box, the Lord will provide."

"You are a fool," she said, but she did so with a smile.

He came over and sat across from her. "And how goes your life?"

She shrugged. "Though the Lord urges us to commit acts of charity, wringing money out of some members of our community is like chipping away at a stone. Very tedious, with little progress. And yet there are many who need help. You should see the line that forms on Friday afternoon at our soup kitchen. There are so many who would go without a Shabbat meal if not for my efforts."

"And I am sure they are appreciated," Ezra said. "In the next world, if not in this one." He leaned over and kissed her cheek, nearly the only physical contact they ever had, and then stood up. "I am going out again. I may not return this evening."

"You have your life," she said, and returned to her letter.

He carried his bag upstairs, transferred a few items to a smaller one, then hailed a carriage to Silas's rooms, hoping to find him in. He was, reading some kind of journal, but he was so happy to see Ezra that he nearly jumped into his arms. Ezra kissed him, with much more interest than he had shown his wife.

"It is a rare lovely day," he said, when they had pulled back. "Too nice outside to stay in. We should walk around the city together. I should like to spend some time getting to know your personality, aside from what I have learned of your body."

"As you wish," Silas said with a smile. "I'm very glad you have returned."

From Silas's rooms they strolled toward Regents Park. "Tell me something about your childhood," Ezra said, as they walked.

"I was a good student, when I could go to school," Silas said. "I was quick to learn my letters and my mother helped me practice my handwriting. In school we had to recite our times tables repeatedly until we memorized them, and I was one of the first to finish." He smiled proudly. "My mother had aspirations for me. She wanted me to be a shop clerk, to wear proper clothes every day and not work in the fields or the mines."

"What did your parents do?"

"My mother took in washing, and my father was an ostler at an inn nearby us. Always came home smelling of horse dung. My mother used him as an example. To grow up to be better than him."

"And you have, working as a law clerk."

"No thanks to either of them," Silas said. "It was all down to the father of my friend, the one who had his way with me. He got me apprenticed to a barrister, and it was my hard work that brought me this far."

He turned to Ezra. "What did your father do, back in Tours?"

"He began as a peddler," Ezra said. "Boats would come up the Loire from the port at Nantes, carrying cargo for men like my father to purchase and then resell from carts. He was hard-working and cut good deals, and eventually he was able to open his own store selling linens and silks. His cousin owned a similar operation in Paris, so when I was in my teens he sold the store in Tours and became a partner with his cousin."

"And you have done well for yourself," Silas said.

Ezra shook his head. "Not in my father's eyes. He does not consider boxing an honest living, because it involves gambling, which people do for the love of money. And it has ruined many a man. And not only that, but I work with my fists rather than my brains. I was never a scholar like you. I can only read and write because my teachers beat the skills into me. I am a great disappointment to him."

"But you are so successful!" Silas said. "Everyone at the arena talks of you and your talent."

Ezra laughed. "My father has never seen me box, and never will."

They followed one of the serpentine paths through the park and suddenly Silas noticed a puppet show ahead of them. He tugged on Ezra's arm. "Let's go watch!"

They arrived at the edge of the crowd, and Ezra made sure to stand a foot apart from Silas so no one would think they were together. Children sat in clusters before the stage, while adults of all ages stood beside them. Instead of Punch and Judy, though, there were four puppets on the stage, talking to each other and moving about.

"See, the large woman all in black is Queen Victoria," Silas whispered, leaning toward him. "I bet the court jester by her side, with the juggling balls, is meant to represent Disraeli. His right leg is lifted to show how he dances to her tune."

"Who is the man in the toga?" Ezra asked. "Those are the colors of the French flag."

Silas studied the puppets as they moved around the stage, and the men who were manipulating them spoke. "I believe that the man in the fez who looks like an organ grinder's monkey is supposed to be the ruler of Egypt. And see, the waves below them? That must be the Suez canal. So the man in the toga represents the president of France."

"Such a spectacle would not be allowed in Paris," Ezra said. "They are poking fun at the governments of three countries, are they not?"

"They are. It is a cornerstone of Britain that we are allowed to argue about our government and its policies. Here they must be fighting over the transfer of ownership of part of the canal from Egypt to England."

"I thought France owned the whole thing. We built it, after all."

"But the Egyptians owned the land surrounding it," Silas said. "Now hush, let's listen."

He crowded next to Ezra and leaned forward, absorbed in the story. Ezra enjoyed the feeling of Silas's body next to his, and the promise it held of their own kind of recreation later. But he was still wary of being too open with so many strangers around them.

Eventually the story ended, with the puppet Disraeli showering the pasha with a rain of paper coins, in exchange for a piece of paper that deeded the Egyptian ownership of the canal to Britain. The crowd cheered and a ragged man passed a hat, collecting coins. Ezra threw in two bronze halfpennies.

"You are a generous man," Silas said, as they walked away.

"I pay for what I enjoy," Ezra said. "Be it food or drink or clothing or entertainment."

"And shall I entertain you later back at my rooms?" Silas asked with a smile.

"You may. But I will pay for your dinner in advance of the entertainment."

They left the park and were passing along Cleveland Street when a man in ragged clothes approached them and handed them a flyer, then hurried off. "What is this?" Ezra said.

"My word," Silas said. "An all-male brothel. And here on Cleveland Street!"

Ezra stopped in his tracks. "Why would someone give something like that to us?"

Silas shrugged. "Maybe he saw something in the way we walked together. But it is nothing, Ezra. We will toss the paper away and no one is the wiser."

Ezra shook his head. "You don't understand, Silas. I must be very careful. If word ever got back to Rebecca that I was … doing the sort of things we do together, it would be the end of our marriage."

"But you have said that you don't bed her."

"No, I don't. But that is our secret, and ours alone. If it were to come out in the community that I am the kind of man I am, we would both be shunned. Rebecca would lose what she has built among the gentry, and her positions in charitable organizations. The shame would drive us both away. We might have to return to Paris. Or worse, Tours."

He stopped. "There was something about that man, the one who gave us the flyer. I think I recognized him."

"You couldn't," Silas said. "One man, on a London street?"

"No, once you read the flyer, it came to me. His name is Israel

Kupersmit. There was a terrible scandal about him as Rebecca and I moved to London."

Ezra began moving quickly. "I must be sure it is him."

Then he stopped. "No, I cannot risk that he recognized me."

"Ezra, you are confusing me. Who is this man?"

"He was a promising young scholar at the Aldgate synagogue, a pupil of the great Rabbi Adler, the Chief Rabbi of the British Empire. Until he was revealed to be a sodomite, and sent from the rabbi's side. He was shunned by the community, struggling to live by begging for change. I have not seen him for several months, but I am sure that was him."

He shook his head. "He must work in that brothel now." He looked at Silas. "What if he recognized me, Silas? Suppose he returns to the shul and tries to use his knowledge about me to better his state? I cannot risk that."

"What can you do?" Silas asked.

"I cannot see you again, not for a while. Not until I know if there are rumors about me."

Chapter 9

Chocolate Drops

Toby

Toby Marsh's new client arrived bearing gifts. Reginald Archer operated a chocolate shop on Piccadilly, a few blocks from Ormond Yard, and one gray December morning he needed help with a contract written in French.

When Will ushered Archer in, he was carrying a pretty box. "Lord Dawson buys these frequently, so I assumed they were a favorite in your household," he said, offering the box to Toby. "They are my special chocolate drops."

Toby rose from his desk to accept the box and shake Archer's hand. Archer was quite a dapper fellow in a well-cut dark suit with a striped vest and spit-polished brogues. Toby generally worked in shirt-sleeves, and though his shirts came from Sampson and Co. of Oxford Street and his slacks from Beale and Inman of New Bond Street, he felt somewhat underdressed.

"Thank you, Mr. Archer. You didn't have to do that. I'm happy to work with you even without the gift."

"Well, it relates to the contract I need your help with," Archer said. "As I mentioned to Lord Dawson, I plan to import cacao beans from Martinique, and the contract which has been offered to me is all in French. He suggested that you might be able to help me clarify some of the language and ensure that terms are as favorable to me as possible."

"I can certainly try," Toby said. "As Magnus might have told you, I have a degree in Modern Romance Languages, and I have several years' experience in reviewing such contracts."

He motioned Archer to a seat across from his desk, and accepted the contract the client proffered. "If you will give me a moment to read," he said.

"Of course. And do try a chocolate drop."

Archer opened the box and offered it to Toby as he read. Absently, he popped a drop in his mouth, then as the flavor hit his taste buds he stopped. "This is quite delicious," he said. "It is almost as if I am eating a flower with the chocolate."

"That is the specialty of the Martinique buds," Archer said. "The main variety of beans is called Amelonado, and they have a strong aromatic effect due to the specifics of the area where they are grown, around Gros-Morne in the mountainous interior of the island."

Toby took another chocolate drop as he read. Then he motioned Archer to move his chair over and he led the merchant through the language of the contract. There was a great deal of technical material about shipping the beans, to which Archer nodded his head.

When they finished, Toby said, "There isn't anything I can suggest to change as regards the basics of the contract. Of course, if you wish to offer different financial terms I can write that up for you in French."

"No, the terms are acceptable. I just have an inbred distrust of the French, you know, after all the years of The Little Corporal and our wars with that country."

"I am curious. You import the beans. What do you do with them when you receive them?"

"I have a small factory in Bermondsey. My team there use steam powered machinery to grind the beans and a Dutch process to create a powder. I created a special process to mix the powder with dried powdered milk and cocoa butter. I have only been able to work with small quantities so far, but I have received a loan from the Rothschild bank to expand considerably, and move into manufacturing chocolate bars which can be sold by other retailers. That's why I need a greater supply of beans."

"Well, if your chocolate bars are as tasty as these drops, you will have an excellent business," Toby said.

Archer wrote Toby a cheque on his account with N.M. Rothschild & Sons for the time spent on the translation, and then left. Toby found it difficult to stop eating the chocolate drops, and by the time Magnus returned home the box Archer had brought was nearly half-empty.

"You have eaten almost all of them!" Magnus said, when he picked up the elegant box, imprinted with a logo of Sagittarius the centaur cocking his bow. He looked, to Toby's eyes, as handsome as ever, with his dark hair, piercing eyes, and cleft chin. Toby stood to embrace him, leaning up for a kiss as Magnus was a bit taller than he was.

"So I have," he said. "Can you taste the chocolate on my lips?"

"I shall have to taste again," Magnus said, and they kissed deeply. Toby's cock rose to the occasion and he felt Magnus's do the same, pressing against the lower reaches of his stomach. It was a promise of things to come; Toby expected a tutoring client shortly.

"What have you been up to this morning?" Toby asked, as he pulled away from his lover.

"I met with my brother," Magnus said. "Always an awkward session with Ledbury, but we had financial business to discuss and papers to sign."

Magnus's older brother had ascended to the title of Duke of Hereford upon the death of their father. The old duke had been aware of Magnus's affection for men since catching him in flagrante with a stable boy. He had deliberately placed conditions in his will to prevent Magnus from inheriting any of the family fortune. Magnus had been able, however, to steer a lucrative investment in his brother's direction, on the condition that he be included in the profits.

It was that investment that largely allowed Magnus and Toby to afford the house in Ormond Yard, to keep Will and Carlo as house staff, and to entertain regularly. Toby was also able to send money to his mother in Norfolk, so she could continue to live in her home and pay her bills.

In addition, they both provided occasional insights to a contact at the Foreign Office, which did not pay in specie but in referrals for tutoring and translation work for Toby. Magnus also had a small fund from his late grandmother.

"Anything of interest?" Toby asked.

Magnus shook his head. "Tiresome business, but it must be done. There is news, however, from my brother Richard in Ceylon."

"Oh really?"

"He has married." Magnus smiled. "As you recall, my father's will expressly prevented him from marrying his long-time mistress, a native woman known as Janani Banda. He is a much cleverer chap than I gave him credit for. He arranged for a fellow planter to marry the woman, changing her name to Jane Clark."

Toby cocked his head in curiosity. "How did that get around the terms of your father's will?"

"As you know, my father stated that Richard was forbidden to marry Janani Banda, or he would lose control of the plantation. But there was nothing in the will forbidding him to marry a divorced woman called Jane Clark."

Toby laughed. "How wonderful. You and Richard have both been able to circumvent the terms of the old bastard's will."

"Yes, it does show that all three of us are smarter than he believed. Well, with the possible exception of Ledbury, who is still a sanctimonious prig. I can see him grit his teeth every time he sees how much money the investments are making for me."

"Even though he makes a similar amount himself?"

"Even though. But it is no matter to me how he feels, as long as the money continues to flow."

"And I have earned my keep this morning," Toby said. He told Magnus about his meeting with the chocolatier. "He said you are the one who recommended me."

"I was indeed. I stopped at Archer's the other day to buy Sylvia chocolates for her birthday and he mentioned a contract in French he needed help with. Of course I told him of your proficiency with the language."

"That was kind of you, and good business as well. Your father would be quite disappointed in your business acumen."

"Well that among other things," Magnus said. "Soon we must plan for our next soirée. I met Sir Arthur Sullivan while I was out and he asked for an invitation, which I promised him with alacrity."

"It will take a week or so to organize," Toby said. "Shall we plan for not this Saturday, but the next?"

"Capital idea." He smiled at Toby. "One more kiss before I'm off?"

"There is little I can refuse you," Toby said with a smile, and kissed him.

Chapter 10

Janner

Raoul

Raoul fretted around the apartment. John had been gone most of the day, and he was irritated that they had lost many hours they could have shared together.

When his lover returned, Raoul demanded, "Where have you been all morning? With my regular hours at the French embassy and your career as a writer, the weekend is the only time we have together."

John crossed the room and kissed Raoul, long and hard, so that Raoul's anger melted. "Now that I have finished my broadside about the Suez Canal financing, my next will be in support of the Artisans' and Laborer's Dwelling Act," he said, as he poured himself a glass of wine from the bottle of red on the sideboard.

He lifted the balloon glass and swirled the wine, then took a long sip. "Ah, delightful," he said.

"This is the act you were discussing last week at Sylvia's dinner party," Raoul said. "What is it about this act that intrigues you, and Janner?"

"Prime Minister Disraeli's government has proposed it to Parliament," John said. "It will allow local councils to buy up areas of slum dwellings in order to clear and then rebuild them."

"Sounds admirable."

"It is indeed," John said. "It is part of Disraeli's social reform initiative aimed at the elevation of the working class. There are many areas of London that could benefit greatly from new, more salubrious housing. Unfortunately the bill as proposed does not force any council to do so, and many consider it an attack on landlords and an infringement on property rights."

"Does your father have any landholdings in such slum areas?" Raoul asked.

John's father, Earl Badgely, was a wealthy man, with his fingers in many pies. Though his ancestral landholding was in Cornwall, where John had been raised, he also had many commercial interests.

"He does own a few buildings in Aldgate," John said. "I plan to have dinner with him at some point and convince him that there can be a commercial benefit for him in redevelopment. That is generally the way to sway his opinion."

John's relationship with his father had improved over the last two years, since certain details of both their romantic lives had become known. Because of his own affairs, the earl had become more tolerant of John's relationship with Raoul.

"I am concerned about Silas's love for Ezra Curiel," Raoul said. "He is always extolling the man's masculine virtues. Yet Curiel is married to a woman, and I cannot see any positive outcome for that."

"I have watched him box in the past, and even placed the odd wager on the outcome of the match. He has quite the impressive musculature."

"So Silas has said. He seems to relish the boxer's strength."

"He could probably hoist Silas up and spear him on his cockstand," John said. He smiled wickedly. "Now there's an image for you."

Raoul felt his cock harden. "Beller has gone to visit his sister for the afternoon, so we have the apartment to ourselves." Though Beller had accepted Raoul's presence in John's home, the man had the ability to move soundlessly about, and Raoul was often nervous about having physical contact with John when Beller might surprise them.

"Then I say we take advantage of it," John said. "How quickly can you be in the bedroom with your clothes removed?"

"Quicker than you can finish that glass of wine in your hand." He jumped up and hurried into the bedroom, undoing the buttons of his shirt as he went. It was an odd quirk of their relationship that both experienced a thrill when John was fully clothed and Raoul was naked, spread before him like a feast. It was perhaps a play against the old idea of the droit de seigneur, when the lord of the manor could have any local wench he wanted on her wedding night—though in Raoul's case he was certainly no wench.

He tossed his shirt away and quickly kicked off his shoes and socks, then struggled to get his trousers undone, hopping from one foot to the next. He let the slacks pool on the floor and tugged down his drawers, allowing his hard cock to spring free.

Then he had to decide—lay on his back, or his front? Present his cock to John to be ravished, or his ass? He thought of the image Silas had presented, of being spread-eagled on his bed and his arms and legs tied to the bedposts. But before he could make a rational decision —as if reason and logic could be present at such a time—he heard John's footsteps in the hall and flung himself down on the bed, his head buried in the down pillows, his legs spread and his arse open.

"Well, what have we here?" John said, as he walked into the bedroom. "Roses are red and ripe for plucking. I see a beautiful ass ripe for fucking."

Raoul giggled into the pillow as John kneeled behind him flicking his tongue against the rosebud of Raoul's arse. John's long, slender fingers pried apart Raoul's cheeks and John applied himself, rubbing his stubbled cheeks against the softness of Raoul's skin, and Raoul shivered with delight.

"I am a goat," John muttered into Raoul's skin. "A randy goat who will munch on anything."

"I hope that goat has a stiff cock, because that's what I want in my arse."

"All in good time, young man," John said. Though John was only his elder by a pair of years, sometimes they used that conceit in their lovemaking. John pulled his head back, and slapped his palm against Raoul's right ass cheek, then repeated the favor with the left.

Raoul squirmed and panted, and felt the clear fluid that emanated from the tip of his cock become a fountain. "Please, my lord," he said. "Do your kind servant the honor of pressing your cock inside me."

"Since you ask so prettily." John stepped back from Raoul, and a cool breeze swept across his arse, furthering the feeling of emptiness left behind by the removal of John's tongue. He closed his eyes and focused on sounds—John's fingers undoing his flies, the removal of the lid from the jar of oil. He visualized John stroking his cock, pulling back the cap to make sure the tip was well-oiled.

Then the bed sank as John climbed up. "And now for the transit of your personal Suez Canal," he said. "Open the lock and let the warship in."

He put his hands beneath Raoul's waist and hoisted him up, then tickled Raoul's hole with the tip of his well-oiled prick.

"Oh, how you tease and torment me," Raoul said.

"And how you love it." John took hold of Raoul's arse cheeks and pushed forward into his hole, and the sensation was exquisite. The pillows blocked out much of his vision and hearing and he concentrated on the feeling of his arse and what that did to his own cock, which was hard as steel and pressed into the bedclothes.

As John began a relentless motion, in and out, Raoul was pushed into the mattress and then released, and the continuing friction was a glorious sensation rising in his cock. John accelerated his movements, a sure sign that he was about to spend, and Raoul beat him to it, shooting what otherwise might have been a geyser of spend into the coverlet.

Then he shared in John's orgasm as his lover shot off into his ass, the fluid pushing forward where the member could not reach, until Raoul thought it might rise up his throat and come out his mouth.

Of course it did not, and John pulled back and stood up. "What a mess you have made of your clothes," John said, looking down at the floor. "Beller will quite disapprove."

Raoul turned onto his side and smiled seductively. "Beller will not return for a while. Why don't you shed your attire and join me here?"

John smiled. "Because you have been a good boy." Then he stopped. "I am sorry. I know you do not relish being called a boy when we are making love."

Throughout his teen years, Raoul had been at the sexual service of his parish priest, Father Maurice, who had taught him all the ways in which two men could make love. He had called Raoul his *bon petit garçon*, or good little boy. And though Raoul had relished his attention then, when he was a bookish boy who was an oddity to his parents and his schoolmates, eventually he had realized that Father Maurice had been wrong to take sexual advantage of him.

"I know your meaning is different." Raoul waved his hand. "Your clothes, my lord?"

John smiled. This was another part of their play, when John removed his clothes piece by piece, revealing his fair skin and light-colored body hair as an on-stage seductress might. Since he had already removed his jacket and cravat upon arriving at home, he began with his linen shirt, unbuttoning it slowly and making as much eye contact with Raoul as possible.

Then he lifted the hem of his undershirt, revealing a tantalizing glimpse of flesh, then lowering it again. He swayed his hips seductively as he undid his belt—his flies having remained undone, though his cock had retreated beneath the fabric.

He turned his back to Raoul and bent over to undo his shoes. He had a sweet arse, muscular round globes that strained against the fabric of his pants. With his shoes kicked off and his socks removed, he turned back to Raoul and let his slacks slide down his sturdy thighs and well-muscled calves.

Part of his work as Janner involved walking around the city, talking to people and getting ideas and insights, so his legs were particularly strong and shapely. He stood there for a moment in his drawers, letting Raoul admire him, then turned to give him a rear view as well.

Raoul surprised John by quickly reaching over while his back was turned and snatching down the drawers so that they rested halfway down his thighs. "You rogue," John said. He shimmied them down the rest of the way without touching them, then bent over when they reached the floor and seized them up. He leaned over and pressed them against Raoul's nose and mouth.

"Smell my spend, you rascal," he said.

Raoul inhaled deeply. The scent was strong and rather like ammonia, with an overlay of the lavender soap that John used in the bath. It was uniquely him, and Raoul loved it.

Then John hopped onto the bed and rested beside Raoul. He curled his left leg protectively over Raoul and pulled him close, and they kissed deeply, then drifted off into dreamland together.

Raoul's last waking thoughts were of Silas, in the hope that he found the same pleasure with the boxer, for however long it could be sustained.

Chapter 11

Soirée

Silas

It was a rare Saturday night when Ezra had fought early on the ticket, and Silas waited for him in the alley outside the boxing ring in New Cross. He wasn't surprised when the man who exited the building looked nothing like the Hammering Hebrew—because he'd been with Ezra enough to know that he could change his attire and appearance when he didn't want to be recognized on the street.

Ezra had begun going bald when he was in his late twenties, and instead of fighting it with creams and nostrums he had embraced it, shaving his head and oiling it before entering the ring. When he was out with Silas, he wore a gray tweed newsboy cap that fit snugly over his head and a long-sleeved jacket that covered his muscular arms.

He also changed the way he walked when he did not want to be on public display. When he was out and about as Ezra Curiel, he strode forward as cocksure as a rooster, his shoulders up and his body forward. But when they were together, Ezra was much more relaxed, letting his shoulders rest, slowing his gait.

"I am glad you are here," Ezra said to him, when the crowd had left and it was only the two of them. "I have watched Rebecca carefully, and it seems that Israel Kupersmit either did not recognize me, or has not spoken of seeing me near the brothel."

"I am not surprised," Silas said. "To have done so would have implicated him even more than you." He hesitated. "So will you dine with me this evening?"

Ezra smiled. "Dine, and more. But we must still be careful how we appear on the street."

They walked to the Tabard Inn, a dark pub that Silas had frequented with Raoul when both were single. The proprietors were a male couple, though the barman dressed as a woman, and it attracted a very louche clientele, many of whom had very different public lives. Silas hoped that no one at the Tabard Inn would recognize Ezra as the Hammering Hebrew, or that at least they had their own secrets to safeguard.

They ordered ale and meat pies. "You must understand some things, if we are to continue to spend time together," Ezra said. "First of all, my position is a very unstable one. One bad injury, and my career would be over. Rebecca has already begun questioning what I will do when I can no longer box."

"What will you do?"

"I have no idea. I have no head for scriptures, so I cannot return to study. Many men who can no longer box turn to physical work, which strains even further and pays little. I have been putting aside some money each month to invest in funds, with the help of a Jew I know who is good with such things. My hope is that my career lasts long enough, and I put aside enough money, that I can live off those investments."

"I know men who live that way," Silas said. "My friend Lord Magnus Dawson for one. He parlayed his savings from a career in the Navy into railway shares, and they support him and his lover."

"You are friendly with a peer of the realm?" Ezra said. "He is one of us?"

"He is. You could even meet him this evening, if you wish. He and his lover are hosting a soirée this evening at their home. You might be able to get some investment advice, or be able to partake of his railway investment."

"I don't know," Ezra said. "I am not the kind of man who attends soirées with the gentry."

"There will be all kinds of people there," Silas protested. "Mostly men of our ilk, but also artists and musicians and a few of the idle rich."

"And all gentile, I am sure," Ezra said. "You make little note of my religion, but I wear it in my face and in my name. And the gentile world wants little to do with the Jews, unless they can profit from us. They believe us secretly disloyal to the Queen and Crown, and they block us from ownership of land and entry into their universities. We are called dirty, cunning-looking, hook-nosed and unsavory. Our hands are criticized for our thick gold rings on our stubby fingers, and the crisp black hair curling down our backs."

Silas sat back, but Ezra continued. "There are constantly questions about our fitness to serve in Parliament. Look at Mr. Disraeli, born a Jew but converted to Anglicanism, most likely to serve his political ambitions. And yet there are many who refuse to ignore the religion of his birth."

Silas was saved from having to respond because of a sudden explosion of smoke from the kitchen.

The proprietor, a fat man named Oliver Hendricks, was known as Jolly Olly. He was less than jolly that evening as he hurried through the room and pushed open the front door, doing his best to wave the smoke outside. It took a few minutes, and when he finished he faced the room and announced, "Sorry, there's been a problem in the kitchen. No pies for the rest of the night. But we have plenty of fish and chips!"

They accepted the change in their order, and a complimentary second glass of ale. Silas recalled what Magnus had said at the birthday dinner, that he could not imagine hosting a Jew at his home. However the conversation with his friends seemed to have changed his opinion, or at least opened him to the possibility. Silas was confident that his good nature would overcome any prejudice.

"I can only tell you that I believe my friends will accept you for who you are," Silas said. "Here am I, a poor ostler's son from Sheffield, an ink-stained wretch toiling at a barrister's office, and they welcome me with open arms."

"Will there be anyone there likely to recognize me?" Ezra asked. As usual, Silas swooned at his lover's accent, which changed his "th" to zed.

"If there is, they will not want to reveal your secret, as they have secrets of their own," Silas said. "And they are not likely to be a crowd that follows the fights. Much more artistic." He tossed his head. "*Comme moi.*"

Ezra laughed. "There is little I can refuse you, *mon cher*," he said. "As long as you do not refuse me later."

"I never would," Silas said.

The male barmaid brought their food, casting a lascivious glance at Ezra. Even in disguise, Ezra was quite the figure of a man. Broad shoulders, a square chin, a narrow waist and thighs like tree trunks.

His physique was intended to frighten his opponents, and in addition to many surprise punches and feints, he had other tricks. He packed the pouch of his shorts with cloth, both to deflect any direct hits there and cower his opponent into believing he was hugely endowed. He was firmly of the belief that the man with the biggest cock always won, even if those cocks stayed securely in their trunks.

They ate, talking of Ezra's training that day and the calendar of matches he had ahead of him. "I will go back to Paris next month," Ezra said. "My renown here in England has led to offers for bigger bouts and higher purses than I was able to gain before I left."

Silas pouted. "How long will you be away?"

"A month," he said. "I wish I could ask you to join me, but my wife will accompany me, and much of my free time will be spent with my family and hers."

"She is a comforting façade for you, is she not?" Silas asked. "Or do you love her?" He leaned forward. "Do you make love to her?"

"Do you see any squalling brats around me?" Ezra asked. "Or do you think that perhaps I try to make them with her and cannot?"

"There are ways to make love to a woman without risking pregnancy," Silas said.

Ezra laughed. "And you know these ways? Not from experience, I am sure."

Silas sat up straighter in his chair. "I could have been with women, had I wanted," he said.

There was a twinkle in Ezra's eye. "Really?"

"When I first came to London from Manchester, I clerked for a barrister in Spitalfields, and rented a room from the barrister's aunt in Whitechapel."

"A very unsavory neighborhood, to be sure," Ezra said. "Even I would be wary of walking there after dark."

"I did not stay there long. The accommodations were quite unclean, and the landlady's daughter thought she would set her cap for me."

"Well, you are a fine-looking man," Ezra said. "And a barrister's clerk would be a step up for a landlady's daughter living in squalor."

"So she believed. She entreated me several times, lowering her blouse to show me her bubbies, which were quite large." He shuddered at the memory. "She had a red pimple on the right one and all I wanted to do was squeeze it but I was afraid she would take the gesture awry."

Ezra was laughing heartily by then.

"She assured me that she knew ten ways to keep from getting with child and described them to me in great detail. As soon as I had my first pay in hand I found myself a better place."

"And that was the last you saw of her," Ezra said.

"Well, not exactly. She was still the niece of my employer, and she came around the office now and then with baked goods for her uncle. She married a bobby last year, though, so after that she only liked me for my wit."

"As I do. Though I will admit I like you for more than just that."

They laughed and talked throughout the meal. As they walked out, Ezra pulled a cigar from his pocket. "Do you smoke?" he asked Silas.

"No, but I like smell of a good cigar, especially one like yours which carries the scent of cedar wood. My first lover used to smoke one of a similar fragrance."

"This is the man your father surprised you with?"

Silas nodded.

"And it does not bring up unpleasant memories?"

"No. What I recall is his kindness toward me."

They were quiet for a block or two, and then turned onto Ormond Yard. "You don't think your friends will be too fine for the likes of me, do you?" Ezra asked anxiously as they turned into the cobbled street. "I do not usually associate with gentry."

"Both John and Magnus have titles," Silas said. "But they are genuine men, the kind you can rely on to get you out of a scrape or two. Magnus was quite helpful to both John and Raoul. And besides, Raoul is your countryman. You can babble away in French to him if you like."

"Usually the gentry try to stay clear from a man like me, who uses his hands," Ezra said. "Oh, it's fine for you, working in an office. The worst that will happen to you is an ink-stained fingertip. But sometimes no matter how I scrub I cannot get another man's blood from beneath my nails."

"You have only to remove your jacket and you will have every eye upon you, and be bathed in flattery." He put his hand in Ezra's meatier one and squeezed as much as he could. "And I will be beside you."

But Ezra would not be assured. "There is also the matter of my religion," he said. "Though I am not as frequent a visitor at the shul as I should be, I wear my faith plainly on my face."

"And in the absence of your foreskin," Silas said. "Come now. It is not like you to be so uncertain of yourself. You are Ezra Curiel, the Hammering Hebrew. The terror of the third ring."

"I am that," Ezra said. "Well, let us go in, then." He extinguished his cigar on the pavement and squared his shoulders.

The houseboy answered Silas's knock. "Good evening, Mr. Warner," Will said.

"Hello, Will," Silas said, as he took off his coat. "And this is my friend, Mr. Curiel."

Will's eyes were as wide as saucers. "My fella and I saw you fight last year," he said. "You were amazing!"

"Thank you kindly," Ezra said, as he handed the boy his coat.

"Everyone is in the front room," Will said. "Lord Dawson is mixing the drinks, but if you want something he does not have to hand, you may easily call on me or Carlo."

"Carlo?" Ezra whispered as Will walked away.

"His fella," Silas said. "He cooks while Will runs the house."

"Quite convenient," Ezra said.

They walked into the front room, and Toby immediately came over to greet them. He enveloped Silas in a hug and then turned to Ezra. "You must be Mr. Curiel," he said, holding out his hand. "Silas has spoken much of you."

Ezra shook it. "Knowing the way Silas speaks, you have heard of my body and probably little else."

Toby was a man of middling height, with sandy blond hair and a dimpled chin. "Well, we were all curious about your..." he waved his hand toward Ezra's crotch. "Religious affiliation."

Ezra turned to Silas in mock anger. "Is there to be nothing sacred between us?" he asked. "Will every man here know I am missing my foreskin?"

It was only then that both Silas and Ezra realized that the room had quieted and that all the men present had heard what he had said. Ezra's face reddened and he was ready to bolt when another man piped up, "Cheerio, old chap. You're not the only one here missing a flap of skin."

Silas recognized him as Gerard Houghton, who ran a men's clothing store on Oxford Street. He was a hefty fellow, with the shadow of a dark beard and hair of a similar color on his knuckles. "Not a member of your illustrious religion, however," Houghton said. "My father was a doctor and he was convinced it was more sanitary to relieve me of it at birth. I have spent a lifetime examining cocks to see what I am missing."

The room laughed, and conversation began again. Magnus Dawson, a tall, handsome, dark-haired man, approached with two glasses of gin. "For you, Silas," he said, handing one glass to him.

"I have another here, if you would like it," Magnus said to Ezra. "Or we have wine and whisky."

"Gin is fine, your lordship," Ezra said. He was sure from the man's bearing that he was the titled one, despite the fact that he appeared to be serving as bartender.

"Please, call me Magnus," he said as he handed the glass over. "Welcome to our home. I must admit to being an admirer of yours, if I may say, without appearing to fawn. Toby is not a fan of the manly arts, but I have accompanied Will and Carlo on occasion to the fights. You have a marvelous right hook."

Silas could tell from Ezra's body language that his lover was relaxing. They spoke to Magnus and Toby for a few minutes, and then moved around the room. When they reached Houghton, the doctor's son said, "Do you find that men will want to suck you as a curiosity? To see what a man tastes like without a foreskin?"

"I have found that," Ezra said. "Though more back in France than here in London. I grew up in Tours, to the south of Paris, where there was a cluster of my countrymen. I went to a Judaic school there until my father moved us to Paris, and so most of my encounters were with boys in a similar state to myself."

Silas had heard little of Ezra's boyhood. "Did you compare cocks with many other boys when you were young?"

Ezra shrugged. "We swam in the backwaters of the Loire when we were boys," he said. "And sometimes the gentile boys would chase us and pull down our pants to laugh at us."

He smiled. "Those boys made me the man I am today."

"How so?" Silas asked.

"I wanted to grow strong enough to defend myself. So I found an old Greek man who had what he called a gymnasium, a place for young men to exercise and grow stronger. Every day after school I would go to him, and he gave me weights to lift, and showed me the rudiments of boxing and self-defense."

He smiled, and Silas could tell he was remembering those days. "It was intoxicating to me that I could train my body in the same way that my schoolteachers were attempting to train my brain. Only the body work came more easily to me. By the time we moved to Paris I was already boxing as an amateur, and in Paris I found it easier to train and improve, and quickly I became a professional."

He drained his glass of gin. "Without those boys and their curiosity, I might never have found my métier."

Silas and Ezra were drawn into a conversation later as John spoke about his newest broadside. "The Artisans' and Laborer's Dwelling Act, passed last year, had a great purpose, but of course there is always opposition to progress, and to anything that benefits the lower classes at the expense of the wealthy," he said.

He turned to Magnus. "Does your brother own any property that might fall under this act? I am assembling a list of the nobility who could be persuaded."

"I am not familiar with what Ledbury does with his capital these days, but I can tell you that our father did not concern himself with city property. The bulk of his wealth came from the countryside, as well as investments abroad."

"That's too bad," John said. "I am endeavoring to convince my father to be among the first to participate in redevelopment efforts. He owns a block of deplorable properties along Cable Street in

Aldgate under copyhold, which gives the tenants little incentive to improve the properties themselves."

"I am not familiar with that term," Raoul said. "What does it mean?"

"In short, that the tenants have only a copy of the deed, not the deed itself," John said. "It is an outmoded method of land transfer which derives from the feudal system of villeinage which involved giving service and produce to the local lord in return for land. They are going out of fashion, due to the various Copyhold Acts of Parliament."

"The House of Lords will argue that such acts cut at the very heart of the British way of life," Magnus said. "My late father was quite opposed to them. When you take away villeinage, you take away loyalty to the gentry, with the effect that you pull everyone down to the same level."

"And what is wrong with that?" John demanded.

"I am merely stating my father's views," Magnus said. "I myself am of a much more progressive viewpoint."

Silas and Ezra stayed at the soirée long after Silas thought they would leave, because Ezra was such a celebrity to the men assembled there. It was nearly two in the morning by the time they stumbled out of the townhouse and into the cobbled street.

"You appeared to fit in comfortably with the other guests," Silas said. "Did you enjoy yourself?"

"I did. It was nice to be accepted fully for who I am, which is something I have not experienced in the past. My religion was a mere curiosity, not an impediment, as was my occupation."

The air was heavy and damp, and they hurried back to Silas's rooms in Bryanston Mews West. They were both tired and more than a little drunk, so the most they managed was some long, tongue-enhanced kisses before falling asleep.

Silas was later to recall a feeling that all was right with the world that night.

Chapter 12

Excursion

Magnus

Magnus was reading the *Morning Post* over breakfast on Monday when he noticed an article about the death of a Rothschild banker involved in the Suez Canal deal. "Weren't we talking about the Suez at Sylvia's party?" he asked Toby.

"We were. News about it?"

"One of the bankers involved was murdered on Saturday night, outside the boxing ring in New Cross. A man called Nathan Walpert."

"I've told you before that is a disreputable area," Toby said. "I worry about Silas spending so much time there. I know there are refined men who like to frequent the place, but they're just asking for trouble, in my opinion."

"So you think his death is about being in the wrong place at the wrong time, rather than having to do with the Suez?"

"What does the *Post* think?"

"As little as possible, as per their usual," Magnus said. He read, "Early Saturday morning the body of banker Nathan Walpert was found in an alley behind the New Cross boxing arena. Walpert was a boxing enthusiast and according to *Post* sources a regular wagerer on the outcome of matches. It is suspected that he won a great deal of money earlier that evening and that criminal figures noted that, and accosted him in a robbery attempt. Police sources warn that it is dangerous to be seen carrying large amounts of cash in poverty-stricken neighborhoods such as that around New Cross."

"That's it?"

"No, there's more. 'Walpert, 31, was one of the bankers involved in Prime Minister Disraeli's scheme to purchase controlling shares in the Suez Canal. Officials at N. M. Rothschild and Company have expressed their sorrow at his death, but claim it has nothing to do with ongoing negotiations. Walpert is survived by his wife Freya, of Hammersmith. In accordance with Judaic traditions, the funeral will take place today at Willesden Jewish Cemetery.'"

"That is rather quick, isn't it?" Toby asked.

"I had a Jewish friend at Eton, and when his father died he was buried almost immediately," Magnus said. "That apparently is their way."

"Thirty-one, you say?" Toby asked. "And no children?"

"None mentioned."

"Do you think it possible he was one of us? Married for convenience?"

"There is no reason to speculate that," Magnus said. "There are many reasons why couples might choose not to have children. Emotional, financial, biological."

"But the Jews often have large families," Toby persisted. "At least in my experience. It does seem odd that he and his wife should have none."

"As usual, the *Post* raises more questions than it answers," Magnus said, and moved on to the next section.

"Don't forget, John Seales will be here shortly for your tour of the underbelly of London life," Toby said. "We shall see if you change your mind about the common man."

"I can be quite common," Magnus said, and Toby laughed.

John arrived shortly after they finished their breakfast. Will showed him in, and Magnus looked up from the paper. "What in the world are you wearing?" he asked.

Seales wore a pair of black broadcloth trousers, a plain white shirt, and a vest of heavy gray cotton. "You didn't think we were going to talk to the poor in morning coats, did you?" he asked.

"I hadn't thought about it," Magnus admitted. "I don't know that I have anything appropriate to wear."

Toby called Will in. "Lord Dawson needs to match Lord Therkenwell's attire," Toby said. "What can be done?"

Will looked from one man to the other. "His lordship has a pair of disreputable wool trousers left over from his time in the Navy," he said after a moment. "I can find him a plain enough shirt in the closet. And Carlo has a denim vest that should fit. Could you wear your navy pea coat, my lord?"

Magnus knew that Toby and Will were spoofing him and John with the constant use of their titles, but he accepted the jibes in good humor. "If I can still fit inside it," he said. "Carlo's food is quite a lot better than what was served on ships."

Will disappeared to put the clothing together, and Toby turned to John. "Where will you go?"

"As I mentioned, my father owns a block of property on Cable Street in Aldgate," he said. "I think we'll start there, interviewing people about their housing and where they would go if they were displaced."

"And if they would return to new housing in the area," Magnus said.

They spoke for a few more minutes, and then Will summoned Magnus to the second floor, where he was kitted out for a day as a working man.

He appraised himself in the oval cheval mirror, turning right and then left. There was something quite odd about seeing himself attired so differently. "I suppose clothes really do make the man," he said to Will. "I feel different."

"To me you still look like a lord," Will said. "Try lowering your shoulders a bit."

Magnus let his body relax. It was hard, after years of discipline to stand up straight, and then all his time in the Navy when he had to be seen as a commander of men.

"Now look down," Will said. "Imagine yourself talking to your father."

"That's not a happy thought," Magnus said. Will had been a boy in the household of the late Duke of Hereford, Magnus's father, and was familiar with the old man's imperious behavior. Magnus pursed his lips and cast his eyes downward.

"You're getting there," Will said. "Just imagine you're always talking to your betters."

When he returned downstairs, John appraised him. "Your hands are too fine," he said. "Give me your right hand."

Magnus did as he was bidden, and John dipped it down to the soil of a potted Boston fern. "There. Now you have a bit of dirt under your nails. And you must try to bring your language down to that of the common man. But you will do. Have you any spare change or small bills?"

"I have some in my change purse."

"Bring that, then, but leave your wallet behind. We may need to spread a few coins to get folk to talk to us."

They bid goodbye to Toby and walked out to Ormond Yard. The air had a chill but it was more bracing than frigid. "You have some experience of this," Magnus said.

"I do. My broadsides as Janner began first to sway opinion regarding various bills in Parliament. But as my audience grew, so did my awareness of certain elements of life about which I have strong feelings."

"Your series about how children are oppressed in factories," Magnus said as they walked. "I read those."

"That was when I first began to do research," John said. "And each child or woman I spoke with gave me new insight into the horrors they face. I believe those interviews helped me make an impact. If people are presented with details of human suffering, they are more likely to respond, either with their votes or their wallets."

They walked to Duke of York Street and hailed a carriage to Cable Street, where they disembarked several blocks ahead of Earl Badgely's properties. "Wouldn't do for us to pull up in a carriage and attempt to be regular folk," John said.

The street was crowded with peddlers, workingmen and women. It smelled of smoke and fish, and there was a constant clatter of sales patter and the clomp of horses' hooves. Magnus did his best to keep his head down and blend in. He found that his attire helped, particularly the bowler hat he had borrowed from Will, which he never would have worn otherwise.

John stopped an elderly woman carrying a full basket of washing. "Here, missus, let us help you with that," he said, in an accent quite unlike his own.

He took one handle of the basket and Magnus the other. It was surprisingly heavy. They followed the woman down the street to her residence, and Magnus could tell from John's raised eyebrow that it was among those of their destination.

They carried the basket inside and up three flights of steps. "Ye're very kind," the woman said. "Can I offer ye a glass of water?"

They both accepted. Magnus was surprised how winded he was after the climb.

John took the opportunity to ask the woman questions about the rooms where she lived, her rent, and the neighborhood. Magnus marveled at how easily John spoke to the woman and the rapport they developed between them.

She sent them down one flight to talk to a young mother with two infants, and to his surprise Magnus found himself rocking one of the babies in his arms to quiet her so that John could talk to her mother.

Before they left, Magnus gave the woman a farthing to buy something for the children, which she accepted gratefully.

That was how the rest of their morning went. After each interview, John took notes of what he had learned, often asking Magnus for his opinions or to clarify something someone had said.

"You should have brought Toby instead of me," Magnus said at one point. "He has much more of an ear for language than I do."

Indeed, some of those they spoke with were recent immigrants from Eastern Europe, who spoke little English, and what they did was often difficult to understand.

"Toby has more experience with common folk than you do," John said. "It's more important that you learn what he already knows."

"He did not grow up in poverty," Magnus protested. "His father was quite wealthy when Toby was a boy, and sent him away to school, and then to Cambridge."

"There is still a difference," John said. "I see it with Raoul. Things that I take for granted are marvels to him. Part of it is the difference in culture between France and Britain. But in the end it all comes down to money. Who has it and who has not."

They stopped an oyster-seller and bought three oysters with bread and butter for each of them. They stopped at a pub for a shandygaff, a mixture of ale and ginger beer. There was a bit of wind when they stepped back outside, but instead of making the air colder, it swept away some of the smoke and let the sun break through.

By the end of the day, Magnus was overwhelmed with all he had learned, but John was still eager to speak with more people. "I don't see how you do it," Magnus said, shaking his head as they returned to Ormond Yard. "Not just the physical aspect—we have been on our feet all day! But the emotional one as well. We have seen more poverty today than I have in the past year."

"That is because you don't see it," John said. "Just look ahead of us. That man with the heavy cart? That boy running? They are our underclass, and they are all around us."

"It is interesting," Magnus said. "Since I met Toby, and we made our connections with the Foreign Office, we have been much more concerned with wealthy foreigners than with the impoverished immigrants such as we met today. I am awed at what I have discovered under my very feet."

"And today was just a sight-seeing excursion compared to what one can see of London if one really looks," John said.

Chapter 13

Dropsy

Silas

On the Monday morning after the soirée, Silas arrived at Barrister Pemberton's office to find the door locked. That was curious, because Cyril Alderton was usually already there, at his desk with a mug of tea. Fortunately, Silas had his own key, and he opened the door, turned on a lamp, and sat down at his own desk to work.

Robb the errand boy arrived a few minutes later, and in Cyril's absence Silas sent him out to pick up various papers that Pemberton would need for ongoing cases.

When nine o'clock arrived with no sign of Cyril, Silas was worried. He reviewed Pemberton's calendar and discovered that the barrister had an early session at court, so there was nothing Silas could do.

After Robb returned with the papers, Silas took it on himself to send the boy to Cyril's address to see what had delayed him. Pemberton returned to the office at eleven. "Where is everyone?" he asked, as he took off his robe.

"Cyril did not appear this morning, so I sent Robb to his home to fetch him."

Pemberton turned to face Silas. He was a handsome man in his forties, his bulky frame made even more impressive by the robe and wig. He had to return to court that afternoon so he left his wig in place. "What is on my calendar?"

Silas had already reviewed it, so he reminded Pemberton of his court appearance and then a new client appointment later that day. "Robb fetched these papers for you," Silas said, as he handed the mover. "Shall I make you a cup of tea?"

"Yes, please," Pemberton said, and walked into his office.

Silas had just finished preparing the tea when Robb burst into the office, out of breath. "What is it, boy?" Silas asked.

"It's Mr. Cyril," Robb said. "His legs began to swell up like a whale on Friday night. Mrs. Cyril called for the doctor Saturday who tried some treatments for the dropsy, but they did not take, and Mr. Cyril passed away last night."

Pemberton appeared from his doorway. "What is that? Cyril has died?"

Silas handed him the mug of tea. "So it appears, sir."

"We must look after the family," Pemberton said. "Figure out Cyril's last pay and prepare an envelope of cash. You and I shall visit his widow after the close of business today."

"Yes, sir," Silas said.

"And in the interim, I want you to assume the duties of chief clerk. You have been doing excellent work, Silas, and I like to reward that in men. We will have to advertise for a junior to assist you."

He went back into his office, leaving Silas with his jaw open. A promotion to senior clerk? After only two years in the office? It was quite remarkable. He felt terrible that it had come at the cost of Cyril's life, but at the same time he was honored by Pemberton's words and eager at the thought of a pay rise.

He did not expect to make as much as Cyril; the man was twenty years older and had a wife and two children. But surely there would be something extra.

He had to banish thoughts of a new cloak or other finery because there was work to be done. A great deal of it, as a matter of fact, because it became clear that Cyril had been ailing for some time and had not kept up with his own work.

There was the calendar to be reviewed and outstanding invoices to be prepared. Normally Cyril would sit in on the first meeting with a new client and later advise Pemberton on how much work would be involved in the case, with a view toward the proper fee to be charged.

Silas plowed through the calendar, noting places where Pemberton was free and new clients could be scheduled. Pemberton left to return to court as Silas worked.

Then he began preparing invoices, something that Cyril had let slide. He was very careful in writing each invoice, using his best penmanship to describe the work the office had done and the hours taken. The invoices were directed to the solicitor who had brought Pemberton the case.

He was surprised at how Cyril had let the work slide, and how he had been so caught up in his own work that he had not noticed the chief clerk's illness. He had a stack of invoices prepared by the time Pemberton returned, ready for the barrister's review before Robb would deliver them.

Pemberton strode into the office, bringing a gust of cold December air with him. He removed his robe and placed his wig on a stand, then turned to Silas. "What is on our docket for the afternoon?" He rubbed his hands to warm them against the chill air.

"Mr. Wigton should be here shortly with a case for you to pursue," Silas said. Antony Wigton was a solicitor who often brought cases to Pemberton. Solicitors dealt directly with clients, and barristers depended on them to learn everything necessary to carry out the case.

Wigton was the son of a landowner and had read law for seven years at the Inns of Court and then spent two years "reading in chambers." That meant he spent time with a barrister to whom he paid a fee for the privilege. He had spent one year of that time with Pemberton so he was well known to the office. Once he had been "called to the bar," he joined a firm of solicitors, where he spoke with clients and drew up proper forms and did deeds, wills, and contracts.

Fortunately, Silas had taken a few moments out of invoice preparation to review the case. It was a simple one; a retailer charged that a factory hadn't delivered the agreed-upon goods by the expiration of the contract. Silas relayed those details to Pemberton, who nodded.

"If you could review these invoices, sir, I'll have Robb deliver them," Silas said, handing the sheets of paper to Pemberton.

"But these cases were adjudicated weeks ago," Pemberton said, as he scanned through them. "Why weren't they already prepared?"

"The best I can guess is that Cyril was ailing and didn't want to reveal it."

Pemberton shook his head. "I have been remiss. I should have kept up with these details."

"You had cases to pursue," Silas said. "It's not as if you sat around your office with your feet up."

Pemberton laughed. "I can see things will run more smoothly with you at the helm," he said. "And I am grateful for a sense of humor as well."

He went into his office to review the invoices. Antony Wigton arrived soon after. He was in his late twenties, barely older than Silas himself, though he carried himself with the air of a much older man, probably the result of all those years of study.

Silas advised him of the death of Mr. Alderton and his own promotion.

"Sorry to hear about old Cyril," Wigton said. "But good show, you, to be promoted. I'm sure you will do a capital job."

Silas carried a copybook with him and settled in a corner of Pemberton's office as Wigton presented the case. "My client, Mr. Adams, owns a haberdashery in Hammersmith. He contracted with a factory in Leeds to deliver one hundred pairs of men's wool gloves by the thirty-first of October. The factory was unable to deliver the full order. Only fifty pairs by the deadline, and another twelve pairs thus far. Mr. Adams has no alternative but to sue."

"He has the alternative of waiting for the order to be fulfilled," Pemberton said. "Has the factory owner provided any excuse?"

"He says that local authorities raided his factory in early October, forcing him to release twenty percent of his work force."

"Forced him?"

"The workers in question were under the age of twelve. Under the terms of the 1833 Factory Act they could not be employed."

"So the manufacturer could not complete the contract due to the reduction in his work force," Pemberton said.

Silas wasn't sure if he was allowed to speak, but there was no time like the present to test the waters. "And presumably this manufacturer was aware that he was breaking the law by hiring children," Silas said. "Which means, does it not, that upon signing the contract he knew there was a chance he would not be able to fulfill it."

"Excellent point, Silas," Pemberton said. "Please make a note of that, and research the appropriate law for me to quote from."

"Yes, sir," Silas said. He still worried about his ability to do everything in the office, particularly without the support of a junior clerk, but Pemberton's words reassured him.

After Wigton left, Pemberton said, "Take some money from the cash drawer and purchase a basket of foodstuff for the Aldertons. We will carry it with us tonight as we pay our condolence call."

Silas felt a small thrill when he set out for the local grocer's. It was another step up in the office. He knew something of Cyril's tastes from seeing the man eat lunch every day—thick bread, slices of ham and cheese with pickle. He was careful to buy items that he thought would last, because back home in Sheffield he had seen neighbors prepare all manner of food to deliver to the bereaved. He wanted his basket to still be usable when the other dishes were finished.

That evening at the close of work, he accompanied Pemberton in a carriage to Cyril's home on Denbigh Street in Pimlico. It was a simple apartment of three rooms, and Mrs. Alderton was in the parlor, being comforted by neighbors, while her three children were sequestered in the back room with an aunt.

Silas admired Pemberton's grace as he spoke with Mrs. Alderton and presented her with Cyril's last pay, as well as some extra to help in the coming weeks. "How will you manage?" he asked her gently.

"My sister lives in Battersea, and she cleans an office building at night," she said. "She has said that the children and I can come live with her for a while, and she will get me a similar kind of job." She dabbed at her eye. "It's nowt what Cyril would have wanted for us, but he's gone and I must make the best of it."

"You must feel free to contact us if you need help," Pemberton said. "You have heard Cyril speak of Silas, I am sure. He will look after you."

"Cyril always said you were a kind man, Mr. Pemberton," Mrs. Alderton said. "In spite of the things people said about you."

She raised her hand to her mouth and her eyes opened wide. "I shouldn't have repeated that."

"It's all right," Pemberton said. "Ours is a difficult business sometimes, and people will complain."

Silas knew the things Mrs. Alderton referred to, and they had nothing to do with business, but Pemberton smoothed things with her. They left soon after, and Pemberton hailed a carriage.

"I can have the driver drop you at your lodgings," Pemberton said. "You are still at Bryanston Mews West?"

"I am, but I can walk, sir," Silas said. "There is no need."

"I would like to speak with you privately," Pemberton said, and Silas followed him into the carriage. The driver, outside on his seat, could not hear them.

"With regard to what Mrs. Alderton said," Pemberton began.

Silas interrupted him. "With all due respect sir, I heard those rumors myself. If you will recall, I first met you at a soirée at the home of Lord Magnus Dawson and Mr. Toby Marsh, who have become close friends of mine."

Pemberton cocked his head. "Usually I have a good recollection of events," he said. "I must have consumed a great deal of gin that night."

"Nothing untoward happened," Silas hurried to say. "I introduced myself and asked about the position of junior clerk, and you invited me to come by the office on the Monday and apply directly."

"That I recall," Pemberton said. "So you have no problem working for a man of my disposition?"

"It would be hypocritical if I did," Silas said. "Since I share the same disposition."

"Well, then, that is fine. And a handsome young man like you, you must have many lovers."

Silas blushed. "Only one at present. He is a boxer, and though he is married to a woman, we have become quite close to each other."

"That is very good," Pemberton said. "I was too devoted to the development of my career to lock myself down with someone when I was young, and now I am old and corpulent, and too accustomed to my own ways. There are men who find me attractive, I admit, but I am only interested in them for momentary pleasure."

They talked of Dawson and Marsh, and then the carriage arrived at Bryanston Mews West. "I shall see you tomorrow morning," Pemberton said. "I am glad we had this conversation."

"I am as well, sir," Silas said. He was excited to tell Ezra about his new position. He wanted to tell Raoul, too. He knew that his friend was worried about his relationship with Ezra, and hoped that this news would be a diversion.

Chapter 14

Bet Din

Ezra

Ezra trained hard on Tuesday, but instead of going right home to Hackney, he passed by Silas's office at the Inns of Court and waylaid him as he was leaving work. They bought sandwiches on the street and quickly ended up in Silas's bed, beneath his canopy of colorful scarves.

Ezra liked being with Silas for many reasons. Sex was high among them, but he was also relieved to be with someone where he did not have to put up a front. He could be exactly who he was. And aside from the incident with Israel Kupersmit of the male brothel, he had been successful at keeping their relationship a secret from Rebecca and from the world.

He realized soon after marrying Rebecca that she had her own ways of doing things, and she didn't like to be challenged. For the most part, he didn't care. Let her run the house her way and serve the foods she liked. She insisted that he leave his boxing gear outside where the maid cleaned his shorts and singlets and other clothing items.

He stored the rest of his gear in a shed in the back garden, and he was strictly forbidden from exercising or practicing in the house, even though there was a huge salon he could use.

He was relaxing beside Silas that evening when Silas turned to him and asked, "Do you have sex with your wife?"

Ezra turned to him. "Is that a question you ask all your lovers?"

Silas said, "For the most part, I do not know if a man is married or not when I go with him. And since I have not bedded anyone else since I met you in September, I have no one else to ask that question."

"My wife is a difficult woman," Ezra said. "On our wedding night, after the festivities ended and we were alone in a hotel room in Paris, she announced that she had no interest in bearing children, and as far as she was concerned, that was the only reason for intercourse between men and women."

"Do you think she would prefer the company of a woman to that of a man?"

Ezra shrugged. "I don't know. I was surprised that night, certainly. Though the large part of my sexual education was with men by that point, my developing physique was admired by various women. Most of them were older and more experienced than I was, so I learned my way around a woman's body. I thought that sex with my wife was a requirement."

"She obviously disagreed."

Ezra nodded. "We lived in a small apartment in the Jewish quarter of Paris, close to both our sets of parents. They all began to wonder when they would be grandparents. Even neighbors would approach us with comments or bawdy jokes."

"That must have been awkward."

"It was. So Rebecca and I hatched the plan to move to London and away from everyone who knew us. I had some boxing contacts who could get me fights, and we had the marriage portion Rebecca's father had settled on us."

Silas ran his index finger down Ezra's hairy chest. "I am very glad you made that decision," he said.

"Our plan was to divorce once we were established here. At first I was very unhappy. My only contacts in London at the time were boxers and promoters, so I had no one to call a friend. Rebecca was determined to make her name, and she did that at first through the Bevis Marks synagogue in Aldgate. She insisted that we attend services every Saturday morning, even if I had been boxing the night before."

He sighed. "Over time I gained notoriety for my boxing prowess, and Rebecca became a curiosity on the social circuit, with her beautiful clothes and Parisian manners. She is now loath to divorce me and lose that status."

Silas reached out and took his hand.

"Fortunately, Rebecca quickly became involved in various charitable activities, and we were able to reduce our synagogue attendance considerably. But I grow more and more disenchanted with my life as time goes on. If I am to live with a roommate, I wish it to be a more convivial one."

"One who would share your bed with pleasure?" Silas asked.

"That would be an advantage."

Silas propped himself on one arm. "And would that roommate be a man or a woman?"

"Public life would be easier if I were to share it with a woman," Ezra said. "But I fear that private life would be just as disappointing as it is with Rebecca."

"How does one interview for this position?"

Ezra shrugged. "For now, the position is not open. Divorce is very difficult in England, and nearly impossible in France. And there is the complication of religion."

"Why?"

"Rebecca and I were married by a rabbi, and only a council of rabbis, called a Bet Din, can dissolve our marriage before God. I am afraid that if I bring such an action against Rebecca, she will rebel against me, and reveal our secrets in such a way that would ruin me."

Ezra sighed. "I have broached the subject with Rebecca. I cannot see how she can be happy in our arrangement, but she is, and she has refused any efforts to change things between us."

Silas leaned back against his pillow. "My life is changing," he said. "I hope for the better, but who knows?"

"How so?" Ezra asked.

"I have spoken to you of the senior clerk in my office, Cyril Alderton. He left this earth a few days ago, and I have been promoted to his position."

"That is excellent!" Ezra said. "I am sure you will succeed."

"I am not," Silas said. "I have a great deal to learn, which I must master very quickly."

Eventually, after another round of lovemaking, Ezra left Silas's and returned to Hackney, where he was surprised to encounter Rebecca at home. Usually she spent her evenings at charitable events or dining with other women from the synagogue.

"*Bonsoir*," he said, as he walked into the parlor. She was sitting at a small desk going through her correspondence.

She answered him in French. "Shouldn't you be practicing somewhere?"

"I have already completed my workout for today," he answered, in the same language. It was easier to speak to her that way, because it allowed him to put her in a compartment in his brain that related to the man he was, back in France.

"I am having a group of people for dinner in an hour," she said. "You won't be here, will you?"

"Not if I am not welcome."

She shrugged. "It is your house, too. Even though my father bought it for us."

"No, your father gave you a wedding portion," he said, though it was an old argument. "We used that money to buy the house. Together. And it is in my name. It is as much my property as you are, as my wife."

She shook her head. "I learned of a recent law the other day." In accented English, she said, "The Married Women's Property Act

1870." Then she reverted to French. "It is an act of the British Parliament that allows married women to be the legal owners of the money they earn and to inherit property."

He had not heard of such a law, and made note to ask Silas about it. "I imagine you would have to petition to have the ownership changed from my name to yours. And I would contest that."

"It would not be much of a contest. Your fists against my brains."

"Why don't you simply go back to Paris?" he asked. "Your father would support you. Your friends are there."

"I have made new friends here," she said. "At the synagogue, and in society. If you would go back I could have an independent life here."

"I cannot get the kind of boxing matches in France that I can here. Nor can I make as much money there."

"Then we are stuck," she said. She turned back to her desk. "If you intend to stay for dinner, please clean yourself up and put on your blue suit. You look most handsome in it."

Ezra had nowhere else to go, and refused to cower in his bedroom like an idiot child while his wife entertained at dinner. So he did as she asked, washing away the sweat of his workout and the smell of Silas. Then he donned the suit she requested.

He surveyed himself in the oval cheval mirror. She was right; the suit did make him look handsome. Too bad Silas wasn't here to see him.

He went downstairs to help Rebecca greet the dinner guests. They did not have a regular cook, instead a woman Rebecca brought in to prepare special meals, who came with staff to help her serve and clear.

She had invited three couples from the synagogue, and they arrived in sequence. Ezra had met all of them at one time or another, though several of the women appeared surprised to see him there. He wondered how many of these events Rebecca had sponsored without notifying or inviting him.

He fell into conversation over gin cocktails with an older

Frenchman who had lived in London for many years. "You have no children, I see," Monsieur Cassin said.

"Rebecca and I have not been so blessed."

Cassin leaned close. "My wife and I suffer from the same affliction. No matter how we tried when we were younger, she could not conceive. The doctors tried various tests, but they are virtually ignorant of anything that happens before the baby begins to push his head out."

Ezra nodded. He did not want to lie to the man, nor did he want to explain why they had no offspring.

"It was very traumatic for my wife," Cassin continued. "It is why we relocated to London, away from the prying eyes of family and friends."

"Your story resembles that of Rebecca and myself," Ezra said.

"You must not blame yourself, or your wife," Cassin said. "Children are given to us at the Lord's discretion. My wife was able to train as a teacher and thus satisfy some of her maternal urges. And she has taught, and helped, so many children, many more than if we might have been blessed with our own."

"Rebecca has thrown herself into her charitable work," Ezra said. "She is moved by the plight of so many women and children in need. You have only to hear her speak of her soup kitchen for the Jewish poor to see that."

"Yes, she is much admired in the community," Cassin said. "As are you, for your physical prowess."

"Gifts from the Lord," Ezra said.

Over dinner, Ezra made a point of complimenting Rebecca whenever possible, on her management of the household, her personal charm, and her devotion to causes. "She is a woman of strong character," he said. "As Proverbs says, 'A woman of valor, who can find? For her price is far above rubies.' I have found my woman of valor in Rebecca."

She blushed. After the guests had departed, and the cook and her staff had cleared everything away, she caught Ezra's arm before he went upstairs. "You were very kind to me this evening," she said.

"I do not hate you, or seek to diminish you in any way," he said. "We entered into a marriage contract that while unusual seems to suit us both. As I prosper, so do you, and vice versa."

"It is good to know that you are behind me," she said. "In good times and bad, one hopes."

Chapter 15

The New Lad

Silas

Pemberton began mentioning the available position of junior clerk to the barristers and solicitors he encountered, but while he did Silas worked hard to catch up on Cyril's delayed work as well as all that was necessary to keep the office running.

Pemberton returned to the office from court on Wednesday afternoon, and he said, "One of the barristers whom you might have met through your friends Lord Dawson and Mr. Marsh suggested you should contact Mr. Quintin Hogg who runs a Ragged School. That he might be able to supply us with a junior clerk."

Silas was surprised that Pemberton should mention the association with Magnus and Toby so easily, but then they had already established themselves as part of the same fraternity.

"I'm not familiar with that term," Silas said. "What kind of a school is a ragged one?"

"It is part of an association that teaches the children of the poor," Pemberton said. "Whether their parents be convicts, drunks, or abusive step-parents, as well as deserted orphans. Hogg himself is the ex-Etonian son of a prosperous London merchant. His operation is just off the Strand."

He looked at his pocket watch. "It is close to the end of the day. You might go over to this school and speak with Mr. Hogg. If you can find a worthwhile candidate, arrange for him to meet with me."

"Yes, sir," Silas said, and he set off for the Strand soon after. The address Pemberton had given him was on his way home, and the afternoon was surprisingly sunny, making him feel quite cheerful, like a boy freed from school.

In only the few years he had been in London, the Strand had changed in character. Nearly 500 cramped dwellings had been pulled down to make way for the recent start of construction on a new location for the Royal Courts of Justice, and as he walked he admired the physiques of some of the workmen.

None could compare to Ezra's, however.

He stopped in front of Simpson's Grand Divan Tavern to watch the chess aficionados play the game with their giant pieces and boards. He had no idea of the rules, but it was jolly to watch the beady-eyed men concentrate, then triumphantly move a piece from one square to another.

He finally reached the address he sought on York Place, in what had looked to have once been a square brick warehouse. He opened the front door to find a maze of small rooms ahead of him. A young woman in a gray dress sat by a table. "May I help you, sir?" she asked.

He explained his mission, and she fetched Mr. Hogg. He had a long, narrow face, accentuated by a mustache and goatee, and dressed like a gentleman, despite the poverty of his surroundings. He did not look to Silas like someone who would be at home in the louche surroundings of Ormond Yard. But in his time as a single man, Silas had met many men who kept that side of themselves hidden, as Ezra did.

Hogg looked him up and down, and Silas wondered if he saw signs of Silas's proclivities, and worried for a moment the man might think he was there to procure a boy for sexual purposes.

"Good day, sir. I work for Barrister Pembroke at the Inns of Court, and it was suggested that I contact you regarding our need for a junior clerk. One who can read and write and do sums."

Hogg appeared satisfied with what he saw, and Silas's statement. "Our mission is to provide free education, food, clothing, lodging and other home missionary services for poor children," Hogg said. "We are called ragged schools because we educate children in worn-out clothes who rarely have shoes and do not own sufficient clothing suitable to attend any other kind of school."

"An admirable undertaking," Silas said.

"We put an emphasis on reading, writing, arithmetic, and study of the Bible, though I often work with exceptionally bright young boys to prepare them for commercial work such as bank and legal clerks. So you have come to the right place."

"Do you have a boy who might fit the bill, to start as soon as possible?" Silas asked. "Or not a boy, exactly, but a young man?"

He worried that if Pemberton brought a boy under the age of puberty into the office, there might be whispers of impropriety.

"Would you have any problem with a lad of Irish extraction? A Catholic?"

"As long as he speaks English clearly there would be no problem."

"Oh, our Luke has been here since he was a small boy, so his English is very clear. He still has some rough edges, mind you. That comes from growing up on the street. But I think he might suit you." He turned to the young woman. "Agnes, could you fetch Luke O'Shea for me? I believe he is in the back classroom."

"Luke is a good lad," Hogg said when the young woman was gone. "A bit too delicate for hard labor, and too sharp as well. I think he would flourish in a barrister's office. Particularly one led by Mr. Pemberton."

"Do you know him, sir?"

"I believe we have met on occasion," Hogg said. "I could not say more than that."

Could not, or would not, Silas thought, establishing more clearly to himself that Hogg had been to Ormond Yard not as a patron of the arts, but as part of the set of men who rejoiced in the company of other men.

Not all of them carried out those desires, he knew. For some, it was enough to simply be around others who shared their tastes, and then go home to their ordinary lives. Or others could be like Pemberton, who had retired from activity and settled for appreciation instead.

Silas hoped he would never end up that way. Though in his deepest heart he accepted that he could not see himself with Ezra in old age.

Agnes returned with a lanky lad, all knees and elbows, with a shaft of blond hair and piercing blue eyes. "This is Luke," Hogg said.

Silas stuck out his hand. "Silas Warner," he said. "Pleased to meet you."

The boy's hand was like a damp fish. That was something he would have to be taught. "If you wouldn't mind sitting," Silas said, and pointed to the desk Agnes had vacated. He ripped a page from his notebook and handed it, and a pencil, to Luke. "Could you please write out the following?"

Luke sat, and Silas dictated a pair of sentences that conveyed documents from Barrister Pembroke to Solicitor Wigton. "And then sign your own name, please."

Luke wrote, and Silas was pleased. He gave the lad an addition exercise and he did not have to frown or lick the pencil, but quickly carried it out correctly.

"Excellent. Please write down this address." He gave him the office address at the Inns of Court. He knew that Pembroke would be in the office all morning. "Please arrive there at ten o'clock. Should Barrister Pembroke approve of you, you would begin immediately."

"Thank you, sir," Luke said.

Silas continued home, happy that he had accomplished a mission on Pemberton's behalf. It reassured him to know that he had the capability to step into Cyril's shoes. That is, if Pemberton agreed with his judgment.

Thursday morning, Luke arrived at the office at nine-thirty. He wore a simple but presentable pair of trousers and a white shirt that had been scrubbed very clean, and a topcoat that was too large on the shoulders and too short at the back.

He stepped in the door and addressed Silas. "Sorry to be early, sir, if it's inconvenient, but I did not want to be late."

"It's not a problem," Silas said. He stood and shook the lad's hand, and introduced him to Robb, who was at least four years younger. "Wait here."

He knocked and went into Pemberton's office. "The lad is here to apply for the junior clerk's job," he said.

"What do you think of him?"

"Well-spoken, though a bit rough around the edges. He can write and do sums, and Mr. Hogg spoke highly of him."

"Very good. Bring him in."

When Silas returned to the outer office, Luke was visibly nervous. "It's all right, lad, no one bites here," he said. "Come and meet Mr. Pemberton."

He ushered Luke inside and shut the door. "He coming to work here?" Robb asked.

"Depends on if the boss likes him," Silas said.

Robb laughed. "The boss will like him fine," he said. 'You have only to look at his face and his arse to know that."

Silas was scandalized. "Robb!" he said.

"Come on, it's no secret that the boss likes a boy in his bed now and then. Doesn't bother me a bit, though I'm interested in girls, not boys. Mr. Cyril used to talk about it. He didn't like it, but he knew that he couldn't get as good a job elsewhere, so he suffered."

Silas was stunned. It was the first time he and Robb had spoken openly in the two years he'd been at the office, and he'd always assumed that Pemberton's inclinations were a secret he was obliged to keep. Now he worried that he had thrust an impressionable young lad into Pemberton's lair. "Do you think he will..." he asked Robb.

Robb shook his head. "The boss likes to look," he said. "And according to Mr. Cyril, he doesn't want to soil his own nest."

The door to Pemberton's office opened, and he and Luke stepped out. "Luke will be joining us," he said. "Silas, can you get him set up?"

"I will, sir," Silas said.

Though he was glad to have an assistant, Silas discovered that at least at the start, his workload was even heavier, because he had to tutor Luke in everything. Fortunately the lad was a fast learner. But Silas worried that he might not be able to leave the office early enough to catch Ezra's fight on Friday evening.

If he couldn't get to the arena, he'd miss seeing Ezra fight, and perhaps even not be able to see him for several more days.

He worked diligently, with Luke and on his own, and on Friday evening he was able to leave at seven o'clock, and hurried across town to the boxing ring. Once again, he was too late to get up close, but he knew that he'd be able to meet Ezra afterwards in the alley.

He joined the jostling crowd for the last match before Ezra's, and was delighted to see his lover march out to the ring along with his opponent. But then everything ground to a halt as two uniformed bobbies stepped up to speak to the referee. "Unfortunately, this match must be cancelled," the referee said, to the accompaniment of boos and catcalls.

Silas was confused—until the referee led Ezra out of the ring and into the custody of the two bobbies.

Chapter 16

Courage

Silas

Silas watched in despair as the police led Ezra away. He spoke to the men around him, but no one had heard any rumors of fight-fixing involving the Hebrew Hammer, or any other allegations that might have led to his arrest. The referee quickly called the next fight on the card, and men hustled to place their bets. Silas fought his way out of the crowd but by the time he got outside, the police had already left with Ezra.

The night was dismal and fetid, the smells of the day close around him. He walked home disconsolately, ignoring the importuning of prostitutes, the rush of carriages, the calls of night birds. He had not felt such despair since his father had discovered him with his pants down.

As he approached his lodgings, he spied the street for any presence of the bobbies. If they'd come for Ezra on charges of sodomy, they might come for him, too. The act of sodomy was a felony punishable by imprisonment and he thought of cases he had read about in his study of the law.

Previous cases had relied on eyewitness testimony of men engaged in sex together, or the presence of feces or spend in bedsheets. But the only place Silas and Ezra had enjoyed each other was Silas's bed, and before he took his linens to the laundress each month, he scrubbed them himself with lye soap to remove any evidence.

Only a dozen years before, up until 1861, all penetrative homosexual acts committed by men were punishable by death. After that, hanging was replaced by life imprisonment.

He tried to think of who might have betrayed them. He had spoken of his relationship with Ezra to only his closest friends—Raoul and John, Magnus and Toby. All four were men of character, and he could not imagine a scenario in which one of them would expose Silas and Ezra.

He should never have brought Ezra to Ormond Yard, he thought. It must have been one of the other guests who had used his knowledge of Ezra to gain favor with the police himself. Any one of them could have been caught, pants down, and negotiated for release by revealing a man of greater renown.

His room, which before had been his place of refuge, held no comfort for him. What good were his colorful scarves, his fripperies, the pictures of Ezra, if they could not protect him?

He stripped down and washed away the sweat and the smell of the boxing ring, which previously would have been intoxicating. Though he climbed into bed he could not sleep.

He tried to reason with himself. What was Ezra Curiel to him, anyway? A casual bedfellow, a chance for fun. The man was married to a woman, after all. Let Rebecca worry about him.

He kept coming back to the question of why Ezra had been arrested at all. Did it have to do with boxing? Ezra had always presented himself as an honorable man. He followed the rules set out by the Marquess of Queensberry. He would never use forbidden moves, nor would he take advantage or hit a man while he was down.

If it wasn't a failure of honor in the ring, what else could it be? He was a very sexual man, so it was possible that he had other lovers, and that he had been caught with one of them—or that one of them had betrayed him.

When dawn broke on Saturday morning, Silas gave up on any pretense of sleep. Worrying was doing him no good. He needed to beard the lion in its own den—to go to Scotland Yard and discover why Ezra had been arrested, and what the charges were against him.

He had seen Cyril go on similar errands, despatched by Barrister Pemberton, so he knew such an effort was possible. He dressed in his best clerk's clothes and set out for Whitehall Place, where a private home which backed onto Great Scotland Yard had been converted into headquarters for the Metropolitan Police.

His nerves overtook him as he approached the two-story brick building, and he stopped at a corner, watching the traffic. In addition to uniformed bobbies, men in ordinary business clothing went in and out of the building, giving Silas hope that he would not stand out. A peddler with a horse and cart passed in front of him, and the horse paused for a moment to leave a steamy dropping on the street.

Silas wrinkled his nose and crossed the pavement to the front door, and then walked inside. He stopped at a desk much like his own, where a clerk sat in front of a large register. "I am from the office of Barrister Richard Pemberton," Silas said, trying desperately to keep his voice from catching. "I am here to understand the charges against Mr. Ezra Curiel."

"The Hammering Hebrew," the clerk said. "I've seen him box. He has a powerful right hand."

Silas relaxed a tiny bit, in the face of a fellow enthusiast. "Did you see him fight against that massive African?" Silas asked. "Big Mo?"

"I did indeed," the clerk said, nodding. "He was masterful."

He looked down at his register, paging backwards one sheet. "Mr. Curiel was brought in last night on the charge of murder."

Silas could not hold back a gasp. "Someone he fought against?"

The clerk shook his head. "The charge is that he committed

murder against the person of Mr. Nathan Walpert. I don't recognize that name, do you?"

"I don't. What an odd name for a boxer."

"A reporter was here late last night from the *Times*," the clerk said. "There may be more in the paper this morning."

"Thank you," Silas said.

"Are you here to register Barrister Pemberton as Mr. Curiel's counsel?"

Silas had to think quickly. He didn't have that authority. "Mr. Pemberton wanted to understand the charges before undertaking a defense," he said. He turned and hurried back out to the street.

It was still early on Saturday morning, but more people were out and about. Maids hurrying to their jobs, workmen in overalls that were mostly clean but would be filthy soon, a boy on a bicycle making a delivery.

Silas spotted a nearby coffee shop called Farr's, and he retreated there to think about his next move over a pint of coffee and two thick slices of bread with butter. He spotted a copy of the *Times* abandoned on a neighboring table, and picked it up. He paged through it until he found a brief announcement of arrests the previous evening. There was nothing more than Ezra's name and that of his victim.

He had been to Barrister Pemberton's home once before, delivering papers that were necessary for an early morning case, so he knew where his boss lived, in an apartment block on Tilney Street adjacent to Hyde Park. He could not bear to think of Ezra in gaol, so he knew he could not wait until Monday morning to ask for Pemberton's help.

The decision, and the strong coffee, gave him renewed strength, and he strode confidently down Pall Mall and through St. James Park. Early morning riders were exercising their mounts, and peddlers and other workers were out about their business in the faint sunlight.

Ladies and gentlemen were already strolling along the park's many walkways, nodding to each other with stiff necks and imperious looks, though they ignored Silas. They could tell from the cut of his coat alone that he was merely a clerk, and not worth their notice.

His courage faltered when he reached Hyde Park and the entrance to Tilney Street. Ahead of him, he saw the impressive white marble of the building where Pemberton lived. Would Pemberton remonstrate him for disturbing his Saturday morning? Could he even be let go for his impertinence?

But then he recalled that part of Cyril's job had been to seek out clients for Pemberton and recommend them. He knew that Ezra had money to pay for his defense, and he could think of no reason why Pemberton should decline to represent him.

He walked slowly up to the building, and was glad to see the porter outside, sweeping the sidewalk. "I work for Barrister Pemberton," Silas said. "I am here to see him."

The porter looked him up and down, then nodded. "He's on the second floor on the right."

"I know. I have been here before. Thank you."

Silas climbed the round staircase and paused in front of Pemberton's door. What if the man had an overnight guest? Silas was aware of his disposition, but realized he knew little of Pemberton's life. He might even have a lover.

He had come this far. He could not fail Ezra. He lifted the lion's head door-knocker and let it ring against the wood.

A few moments later, Pemberton opened the door, wearing a long cotton robe. "Silas. What's the matter?"

Silas opened his mouth, but no words would come.

"You'd better come inside," Pemberton said.

Pemberton led him to the kitchen, which had a small table suitable for two. Pemberton put the kettle on and then poured Silas a cup of tea, and then one for himself. "Now then, my boy, what is the matter?"

"It's Ezra Curiel, sir," Silas said. "He's been arrested for murder."

"The boxer," Pemberton said. "How did you hear about this?"

"I was at the fights last night when the bobbies came for him,"

Silas said. "I went to Scotland Yard this morning and discovered the charge against him, which is also in the *Times* this morning. Can you represent him, please? I know he's innocent."

"How can you know that?" Pemberton asked.

"Because he's my lover."

Pemberton took that news in stride. "Well, you can certainly testify to me of his character, or your experience of his character. Sir William Garrow coined the phrase 'presumed innocent until proven guilty,' which is something I have long believed. But we would have to know a great deal more about the charge against him before we establish that as concrete in this case."

"Does that mean you'll take on his defense?" Silas said. "He has money to pay, I know. He has ever been generous with me, and he maintains a household in Hackney. He told me that he purchased the house for cash."

"It is what I do," Pemberton said. "I believe that every man deserves a defense against charges. But you know that I cannot engage with Mr. Curiel myself; the job must come through a solicitor. Why don't you present your case to Mr. Wigton and see if he will agree to represent Mr. Curiel?"

"But it's Saturday," Silas nearly wailed. "I won't be able to go to Wigton's chambers until Monday morning."

"You know where he lives," Pemberton said. "And you know the law does not keep regular hours when a man is in jeopardy."

Silas remembered that when Wigton spent a year in Pemberton's office, he'd had reason to deliver papers to him at his apartment—not far from Bryanston Mews. "I recall where he lives," he said.

"Go to see him, tell him that you and I have spoken, and ask him if his firm will represent Mr. Curiel."

He pursed his lips. "It may be necessary at some point for you to reveal the nature of your relationship with Mr. Curiel to Wigton, but for now I suggest you maintain that you are an aficionado of the fights and particularly of the Hebrew Hammer, and recognize that this might be a lucrative opportunity for both of us."

"I will do that, sir. And thank you."

"You are my senior clerk now, Silas. You must get accustomed to this role. This is the very thing you are meant to do. Now hurry, before Wigton goes off to enjoy his Saturday."

The sun was well up by that time, and the London streets were crowded as Silas hurried to Wigton's apartment. He shared a suite of rooms with two other young solicitors in a much nicer building than Silas's own, though several steps down from Pemberton's.

He rang the buzzer, and the door opened. He walked into a foyer tiled in black and white, and a staircase like the one at Pemberton's before him. He climbed to the third floor and found a door ajar. He knocked, and a young man he did not know came to the door, in a pair of trousers and a white shirt, with suspenders that had not yet been fastened.

"Yes?" the man asked.

"I'm here to see Mr. Wigton, if he's available."

"Antony!" the man called back into the apartment. "A boy for you."

Silas swallowed a comment. He was hardly a boy; he was the same age as the man before him. But he was a clerk, and the man was a solicitor, so he was a boy, and he'd remain so until he died.

The man with the suspenders walked away, and Silas hovered on the doorstep until Wigton appeared. He looked much younger without his suit on, and it was clear that he had not shaved that morning, and his blond hair was quite tousled. "Silas," he said with surprise. "What brings you out on a Saturday morning?"

"It's a case, sir. Barrister Pemberton thought you might be willing to take it on, and that he would arrange the defense."

"Well, then, come inside and tell me the details."

The lounge was quite disheveled—several pieces of male attire, and a woman's brassiere, were scattered over the furniture. Several empty wine bottles and dirty glasses were on the coffee table.

Wigton said, "Excuse the mess. My flatmates had a bit of a party last night." He gathered the clothing and tossed it into a pile in the corner, and motioned Silas to a seat. "Tell me about the case."

Silas recited what he knew, from Ezra's arrest the night before to his visit to Scotland Yard and to Pemberton's home. He said only that he was an acquaintance of Ezra's, as well as a fan of the fights.

Wigton rubbed his hands together in glee. "This sounds like an excellent case, and one that could bring us some notoriety," he said. "Good work, Silas. I'm very glad you brought this to my attention."

Wigton promised to visit Ezra at Scotland Yard and glean what he could about the case, and then would come to Pemberton's office on Monday morning to discuss the terms. Fortunately Silas had memorized much of the calendar, and he was able to schedule a time right then.

Wigton stood, and Silas followed suit. "Leave it to me, Silas," Wigton said. "We'll get the wheels moving."

He left Wigton's apartment with a bad taste in his mouth. The solicitor was too eager to take on a murder case for the benefits it might bring him. Would he treat Ezra as a valued client, or merely as a source of funds?

Silas knew there had to be more he could do, and as he stood in the street and a pair of gentlemen in top hats passed him, he knew where he had to go next.

Chapter 17

Allegation

Magnus

Magnus was reading the Saturday paper in his dressing gown when he noticed the brief article entitled "Boxer Arrested in Banker's Death."

"Boxer Ezra Curiel, the Hammering Hebrew, has been arrested in conjunction with the beating death of banker Nathan Walpert. Walpert's body was found in the alley behind the boxing ring at New Cross in the late hours of Saturday November 28. The coroner has determined that he suffered a severe body blow to the stomach, which pushed him backwards so that he hit his head on the cobblestones. The subsequent injury caused his brain to bleed out and resulted in his death."

He looked over at Toby, who had already washed and dressed, wearing a pair of gray slacks, a white shirt and a wool jumper. "Here, Toby, did you see this?" he asked. "Silas's lover has been arrested."

Toby moved his chair around the breakfast table to read along with Magnus. "A witness placed Curiel at the scene of the crime. Upon being questioned, his wife, Mrs. Rebecca Curiel, told the police that her husband had returned home that evening in blood-stained clothes."

Magnus put the paper down. "Why, that is ridiculous," he said. "Anyone familiar with boxing would know that the men involved frequently sustain injuries which result in blood on their clothing."

"But presumably Curiel did not travel home in his boxing shorts," Toby said. "Wouldn't his wounds have been treated at the ring, and then he dressed in his regular clothing?"

"That is true. But many bandages do not hold, and blood seeps out," Magnus said. "Remember how you skinned your knee last month? Despite our efforts to control the blood it did seep into your tweed trousers."

"And Will had a devil of a time removing the stain," Toby said. "But poor Silas, to have his romantic hopes dashed so terribly."

"Well, we both knew there was little hope of a happy ending between them," Magnus said. "The Mrs. Curiel of whom the article spoke would surely be an impediment." He shook his head. "And now this charge of murder. Surely that will be the end of their affair. Silas will have to count himself lucky if his assignation with the boxer is not revealed."

They both sighed, and Magnus resumed reading the paper while Toby returned to his breakfast. Will was clearing the table when they heard a prodigious banging on the front door.

"Whoever is that?" Magnus asked. "On a Saturday morning?"

"I will see to it," Will said. "Probably a peddler."

Magnus heard him open the door, and then hurried footsteps in the hall. Silas Warner burst into the breakfast room. "I need your help!" he exclaimed.

Right behind him, Will looked chagrined. "Mr. Warner," he said.

"It's all right, Will." Magnus rose, pulling the belt of his dressing gown tighter. "Shall we retire to the parlor? We have already read the article in the *Times*, but you may tell us anything else you know."

"I saw him arrested last night," Silas said, his voice rent with despair.

Toby took Silas by the arm. "Will, could you bring Mr. Warner a cup of strong tea?"

Will bustled into the kitchen as the three men removed to the parlor. Magnus brought the paper with him, and handed it to Silas to read.

Magnus felt uncomfortable receiving guests in his gown, so he left Toby and Silas in the parlor and hurried upstairs, where he dressed quickly. By the time he returned, Silas had finished reading the article.

"This is utter falsehood," he said. "I know Ezra and though he's strong, he'd never deliberately hurt someone."

Magnus said gently, "From what the *Times* has written, the coroner believes Mr. Walpert suffered a punch, which knocked him backwards. Mr. Curiel could have delivered such a punch, not realizing that it would send Mr. Walpert to the ground."

"And there is the matter of blood on Mr. Curiel's clothes," Toby said. "Though as Magnus has pointed out that could have been from his injuries in the fight that night."

"That's just it," Silas said. "I was there for that fight, and Ezra won cleanly. He was not injured at all."

"Then the blood must have come from Mr. Walpert?" Magnus asked.

Silas shook his head. "There was no blood. Or you would have seen it yourselves."

Toby and Magnus looked at him curiously. "What do you mean?"

"Look at the date of the banker's death. Last Saturday night."

Magnus said, "The night of our most recent soirée."

"Indeed," Silas said. "I watched Ezra win his bout, and then we met outside the ring. There was no blood on his clothes. We dined together at the Tabard Inn. And then I brought him here directly."

"So you believe that he could not have committed this crime?" Magnus asked.

"I don't believe it, I know it."

"Do we have last week's *Times*?" Magnus asked Toby.

"Will usually saves the papers for kindling," Toby said. "I'll ask him." He walked out.

"This is a difficult situation," Magnus said, leaning forward from his place on the divan. "The police have a witness who places Mr. Curiel at the scene of the crime, at the time Mr. Walpert was hit. And yet you affirm that Mr. Curiel could not have been at that place at that time, because he was with you."

"That's true. But I can't just go to the police and tell them that, can I? It would mean the ruination of Ezra's career, if his proclivity became known."

"Does his wife know of you? Or other dalliances with men that Mr. Curiel may have had in the past?"

"I don't know," Silas said.

Toby returned with the front section of the previous Monday's paper. "It was at the top of the pile, ready to go into the fire," he said.

The three of them clustered together to read the original article. "See, it says that Mr. Walpert was beaten after the last fight of the evening, when the ring had emptied," Silas said. "That night, Ezra was in the first of six matches, before the main event. By the time the last fight was finished, we had already dined and arrived here."

Magnus put down the paper. "So it appears that someone has put Mr. Curiel into the frame, with the assistance of the boxer's wife. Unless all three of us, those who might have seen the two of you at the Tabard, and those in attendance at the soirée, have been fooled, Mr. Curiel is innocent of this crime. The question is what can we do to prove that?

Chapter 18

Assignments

Silas

Silas was sent to fetch Pemberton and bring him to Ormond Yard so they could consider how to help Ezra. He hurried to Pemberton's flat on Tilney Street and knocked on the door once more. This time Pemberton was fully clothed and ready for business.

"I am sorry to trouble you again, Mr. Pemberton," Silas began.

"It's no trouble, Silas. Is there any news about your friend?"

"I spoke with Mr. Wigton, and he has agreed to investigate the charges against Ezra, and with his permission, represent him. I also went to Ormond Yard."

"Ah, yes. Magnus and Toby are good friends of yours."

"They are. And they can substantiate my testimony as to Ezra's alibi." He explained how he and Ezra had been at the soirée at the time of the murder. "Could you possibly come to Ormond Yard to consult with us on Ezra's defense?"

"Certainly. Let me get my hat and cloak." They took a carriage to Ormond Yard.

Toby answered the door. "Will was sent to John's apartment, though he returned with a message that John was out researching, and he and Raoul will arrive as soon as they can." He took their coats and Pemberton's hat and hung them on pegs by the door.

They walked into the lounge, where Magnus awaited them. Pemberton sat, and Silas began to take notes.

"We shall need a great deal of research," Pemberton said. "First, to establish Mr. Curiel's alibi in a way that does not open him to public scorn as man of our ilk. It would be easy enough for the prosecutor to demean Silas's testimony because the sexual relationship between them would be sure to come out."

"Could one of us testify to Mr. Curiel's presence at the soirée?" Magnus asked. "Or would someone use that against him?"

"I'd like to see a list of all the guests," Pemberton said. "I know that you have in the past invited numerous artists and other public figures whose sexual bona fides are clear."

"I can take care of that," Toby said. "Though eventually we would need the guests' permission to reveal that they were with us. What else?"

"We need to identify the witness who says he saw Mr. Curiel in the alley after the fight. To determine why he has made such a statement."

"Obviously under some sort of pressure," Silas said. "It is a serious offense to lie under oath, so this person must have a strong motivation."

"Indeed," Pemberton continued. "We also need to understand why Mrs. Curiel made her statement. Is she under a similar sort of pressure? Or is she angry about her husband's proclivities and sees this as an opportunity to be rid of him?"

"Perhaps our friend the Honorable Sylvia Cooke could be of service there," Magnus said. "She is acquainted with Mrs. Curiel through her charity work."

"Excellent. Now, we must turn our attention to preparation for the trial, should we be unable to provide the police with a convincing alibi for Mr. Curiel."

Pemberton pulled out the article from the *Times* and read aloud:

"The coroner has determined that he suffered a severe body blow to the stomach, which pushed him backwards so that he hit his head on the cobblestones. The subsequent injury caused his brain to bleed out and resulted in his death."

He put the paper down. "If the case comes to trial, we might argue that Mr. Walpert's death was an accidental one. Silas, you will need to do some research for me. Identify other cases in which a death occurred by accidental means. Ideally under similar circumstances—an ill-timed or ill-directed physical assault."

"I can do that."

"Then we need to set up some distractions for the judge to consider. Mr. Walpert was a banker involved in the financing of the Suez Canal acquisition. Could we speculate that his death was somehow involved in that operation?"

"I have a contact with the Foreign Office," Toby said. "I can speak with Gervase Quinn and see if he has any insights that might prove useful."

Pemberton picked up the newspaper again. "There is a gambling angle we might pursue as well, since the *Times* has been good enough to mention the presence of betting at the boxing hall. How can we discern if Walpert was indeed a gambler?" He turned to Silas. "Would you recognize Mr. Walpert? Could you have seen him at the ring?"

Silas thought for a moment. "I have," he said. "I remember he introduced himself as we were waiting for a round to begin, and spoke of betting. And then he called Ezra 'my fellow' which surprised me."

"Could he have been seeing Ezra as you were?" Pemberton asked. "Perhaps Ezra is being framed as part of a lovers' quarrel?"

Silas shook his head. "I thought I saw something in this Walpert's eye, but he said that he thought of Ezra as a co-religionist, a fellow Jew."

"And Walpert's religion was established by the *Post*," Magnus said. "Was he a significant bettor, do you recall?"

"I believe he wasn't very successful," Silas said. "He was reluctant to bet on Ezra because the odds were in his favor. He seemed like a man in search of a big payoff."

"Which is always a bad strategy in betting," Magnus said.

"He did place a wager on Ezra that night, because I said I had been following Ezra's form, and that he was quite likely to win."

"So we have established that Walpert was a gambler, and not necessarily a successful one," Pemberton said. "So he might have accumulated some debts and the punch was a threat against him."

"But why kill a man who owes you money?" Toby asked.

"Perhaps it was an unfortunate accident," Pemberton said. "Another possible distraction away from Mr. Curiel."

By then Silas had covered two pages of ways to approach Ezra's defense. He had helped Cyril take such notes in the past, but he had never felt such a close connection to a case before.

He had the suspicion that Ezra meant more to him than he had previously realized, and that was a dangerous situation to be in. And not just because his heart might be broken, but because he could be drawn into the case personally, with potentially life-threatening consequences.

Chapter 19

Common Man

John

John Seales did not get a chance to read the *Times* that Saturday morning. He was up with the birds, dressed in his common clothes, on a mission to interview more people around Cable Street. It wasn't until he had returned home when he heard from Raoul that they had an urgent summons to meet at Ormond Yard.

"Was there any reason given?" John asked, as he peeled off his white shirt. His undershirt was damp and stained with his sweat, and he wanted a bath.

"None in the note," Raoul said. "But there was an article in the *Times* this morning. Silas's lover has been arrested."

John had just opened his flies and was about to step out of his trousers, which had been stained around the cuffs with mud and fish guts, but he stopped.

"Arrested? On what charge? Sodomy?"

"Worse. Murder."

"Murder? Whose?"

"A Rothschild's banker involved in the Suez deal," Raoul said.

John continued stripping his clothes, since he'd already asked his valet Beller to prepare him a bath. "That doesn't make sense," John said. "What would a boxer have to do with a financial arrangement between nations?"

"Perhaps he was hired to threaten the banker, and things got out of hand," Raoul said. "Or word of the boxer's proclivities reached the police, and this is just a pretense to arrest him."

The news had a negative effect on John; his cock was small and furled against his pubic hair. He realized once more how vulnerable he and Raoul were, as well as many of their friends.

"Take your bath, and then we shall go to Ormond Yard and see what's what," Raoul said. "And perhaps they shall give us a good dinner. I have quite a taste for Carlo's cuisine."

John bathed and dressed and they set out for Ormond Yard. When they arrived, shortly after three o'clock, they found Silas there, as expected. What was surprising was the presence of Barrister Pemberton as well.

Though they had met at a previous soirée, they were still introduced. "At Silas's urging, I have agreed to defend Mr. Curiel in court against the charge of murder," Pemberton said.

John looked at Raoul, who nodded. "We will do whatever we can to help."

Five of them sat in the parlor, fortified by glasses of whisky. Magnus and Toby occupied one sofa, and Raoul and John another. Silas sat by himself, and Pemberton stood beside him.

"Silas, why don't you recap all that we have already thought about?" Pemberton asked, and Silas did so.

"An admirable list," John said, when he was finished. "What can we do?"

"I am going to speak with my contact at the Foreign Office on Monday," Toby said. "Raoul, could you carry out similar questions in the French embassy?"

"I can. There has already been much talk in my office about the Suez deal, but I will ask around for more details and see if the dead man's name comes up."

Pemberton said, "Excellent," and Silas wrote down Raoul's task.

"We may have another connection," Magnus said. "Our friend Gerard Houghton is a regular at the fights."

"The fellow without a foreskin," Silas said. "Yes, I have seen him around the ring on occasion."

"He may know about Walpert's gambling, and who he owed," Magnus said. "I will contact him."

"That is good, because our final task is to determine if there is another viable suspect," Pemberton said. "Perhaps someone who lost money at the arena on Walpert's advice? A fellow Jew who was angry with Walpert for some reason, and tracked him down to the arena and assaulted him? It is a pity we don't have a connection in the Jewish community who could shed light on Walpert's connection to his people."

"I may know someone," Magnus said. "A wine seller called Samuel Steingrob. I have had several pleasant conversations with him in the past. He might know something about Walpert we could not discover elsewhere."

John realized that everyone present had the assignments but him. "What can I do?" he asked.

Pemberton turned to him. "It's my understanding that you have an ability to speak with the common man. You could spend some time around New Cross and see what you can discover about people who hang around in those alleys."

He looked over at Silas. "You have a team around you, my boy. We will all do what we can to establish your lover's innocence without compromising either of you. Neither of you would benefit by serving time in gaol."

Chapter 20

Rabbit

Magnus

It was already evening by the time they finished their plans, and Carlo had recognized that and spent some time in the kitchen preparing dinner for everyone. Will had slipped out and purchased oysters, which were served on the half shell with melted butter and slices of fresh-baked bread.

Carlo had roasted two chickens, which were served with onions that had been sautéed in butter until they were caramelized. Carrots had been roasted and shaved into curls and were accompanied by sliced roast turnips.

"Your cook is truly a marvel," Pemberton said. "Had I a larger household I would be tempted to steal him from you."

"So far he and Will are quite happy with us, and we are happy with both of them," Magnus said. "We shall have to make you a regular guest at dinner in the future."

"That alone would be an excellent motivation for me to secure Mr. Curiel's release," Pemberton said. "I am sure with such an excellent team behind me I will triumph in court."

Carlo had also baked an apple tart, topped with whipped sweetened cream, which left all the guests asking for more.

Finally, they all left, and Magnus and Toby reclined in the lounge with glasses of brandy while Will and Carlo cleaned up. "This has certainly been a surprising day," Magnus said.

"I knew something of the sort would happen as soon as you read out the article in the *Times* this morning," Toby said. "My work is clear. I must fit a visit to Gervase Quinn into my Monday schedule and attempt to insinuate us into any investigation of the deal between the Suez Company and Disraeli. If there is indeed an inquiry."

"I will speak with Gerard Houghton," Magnus said. "I'll send Will around tomorrow morning with a request and see what kind of response I get."

Sunday morning, after a sumptuous breakfast of porridge, fish, eggs and bacon, Magnus sent Will around to Houghton's lodgings, and the boy returned soon after with an invitation for Magnus and Toby to join him for tea that afternoon at three.

When that was settled, Magnus sent a note to Sylvia and Jess asking if he could stop by, and Will returned with a welcome any time that morning. So while Toby remained at home to work on a translation for a client, Magnus set off on foot to the mews off Jermyn Street.

The air had cleared and a bit of sun warmed the chilly air. Magnus tipped his hat several times to well-dressed ladies out for a stroll.

"This is a treat," Jess said, when she answered the door. "We haven't seen you since Sylvia's birthday two weeks ago."

"December is always a busy month," Magnus said, handing Jenny the maid his coat and hat. "How have you been?"

"Sylvia keeps us on a whirl with her charity work. She's in the lounge now, writing out invitations to a party in January."

Magnus and Sylvia kissed cheeks, and Magnus accepted the offer of a cup of tea. "What brings you out?" Sylvia asked.

"Were you aware that Mrs. Curiel's husband has been arrested for murder?" he asked.

Sylvia nodded. "Yes, Jess read that in the paper yesterday. We have been debating what action to take. Whether to send her a note, or try to arrange a visit."

"And that is what I have come ask. We recently learned that Mr. Curiel, the boxer, is an invert. Do you recall meeting our friend Silas Warner at your birthday dinner?"

"The law clerk? A very lively fellow. Yes, I remember him." She looked closely at him. "Didn't you say that the two of them were lovers?"

"They are. And on the Saturday night in question, Ezra boxed in an early match, and then left the arena to dine with Silas at the Tabard. From there, they came directly to our home for a soirée. So it is impossible that Ezra could be in the alley behind the boxing arena at the time of Walpert's death."

"And yet according to the *Times*, Rebecca implicated her husband," Jess said.

"Exactly. Which is why Silas would appreciate it if you could visit Mrs. Curiel and see if you can determine why she would do so, when there is evidence to the contrary."

"What an intriguing puzzle," Sylvia said. "Yes, I think we could arrange to pay a call on Mrs. Curiel to comfort her in this distressing time."

"She is quite keen to continue acquaintance with anyone in society," Jess said drily. "I feel confident we will be received."

Sylvia turned to Magnus. "Why do you think she has lied in this manner?"

"Could it be to access her husband's wealth and establish herself as a woman of independent means?" Magnus asked. "You are both aware of the strictures that come of being a wife."

"And she has expressed to us a distaste in the past about how her husband earns his living," Jess said. "Removing him from the picture could allow her to find a new husband with greater status."

Sylvia shook her head. "She is a Jewess, remember. Short of marrying into the Rothschilds, she is not about to enter society."

They discussed various scenarios over tea and cakes, and then

Magnus returned to Ormond Yard in time to head to Gerard Houghton's. "I think I shall float away on an ocean of tea today," Magnus said.

"It is the British way, after all," Toby said.

Houghton's address led them to a narrow door adjacent to a doctor's surgery on Bond Street. They rang the bell and a young housemaid answered the door and led them up a staircase.

"Welcome to my ancestral home," Houghton said. "The surgery below once belonged to my father. When he passed the practice was sold but I retained the apartment."

He was in his shirtsleeves, which revealed more of the hair that seemed to cover his body—fine, dark ones on his lower arms, and a tuft that peeked out of his open collar. He led them into a fusty salon, one which had not been decorated since before Victoria ascended to the throne. A silver tea service had already been laid out on the table, along with very good bone china—all, Magnus presumed, inherited from the late Houghtons, since none of it reflected the character of the man in front of them.

He poured the tea, and then said, "To what do I owe this honor?"

"You may have read about the fate of the boxer Ezra Curiel in the *Times*," Magnus said.

"Indeed I did. Tragic thing. I suppose that type of man must be violent in nature, to choose a career in the ring."

"The thing is, we have direct evidence of Curiel's innocence," Toby said. "At the very time of the alleged crime, he was at our home." He paused for impact. "Discussing, if I recall correctly, your mutual lack of foreskin."

Gerard put his teacup down on the saucer with a clatter. "Really? How odd."

"You do recall the conversation?" Magnus asked.

"Of course. It is not often that the topic of foreskin comes up in polite conversation. Even at a soirée like yours."

He stared at them. "But you can't imagine that I would give evidence of that in a court," he said.

"Not the particular topic of conversation, of course," Magnus said. "But if we were to need to establish Mr. Curiel's alibi, would you be willing to acknowledge your presence that evening?"

Before Gerard could respond, Toby hastened to add, "While there were several men there who might be called inverts in less polite company, such as Magnus and myself, there were others present as well with sexual bona fides relating to women. So you would not be incriminating yourself by stating you were in our company."

Gerard looked down at the floor and was quiet. Magnus and Toby shared a glance before he spoke.

"I have not spoken of this before, because it is not something of which I am proud," he said. "While other men might boast of sexual exploits I prefer to keep myself to myself." He sighed. "But two years ago I was arrested in the alley behind the Tabard. In flagrante, if you will, with my cock in the mouth of a boy who pretended to be much older than he was."

"Oh, dear," Magnus said. "Were there consequences?"

"I do not come from a titled family, as you know, but my father had some reputation among the police for treating their injuries, so his name and credit helped me. The boy admitted that he had lied about his age, which helped as well. I paid a fine, on my behalf and on his, and the case was dismissed."

Gerard sighed once again. "So you can see I would not like to have my name brought into a case that might position me in a similar light."

Toby and Magnus shared a glance again, and Magnus nodded. "Of course."

"But I may be able to shed some light on Mr. Curiel's defense," he said. "Because I attended the fights the night of your soirée, and I spoke with a man there who was down on his luck."

"Go on," Toby said.

"Though I am not a wealthy man, I am not opposed to putting a few coins in the way of a man who needs it, in exchange for… well, services."

Magnus had never found it necessary to pay for sex. He was lucky enough to be tall and handsome, and have spent many years among sailors who were deprived of contact with the fair sex, and so more willing to exchange favors with each other. And then, of course, he met Toby.

"This gentleman—and he was a gentleman, I could tell from his clothing—had a certain look in his eye. But then he turned and fled from me."

Magnus wasn't sure where this conversation was going, but he nodded encouragingly.

"I gave him a few minutes' head start, and then followed him out of the ring. I spotted him in the alley, talking to a much larger man. I was disappointed, of course. I assumed my instincts had been right, but I was too slow to respond, and another man had gotten in first."

Magnus was spellbound, eager to hear what happened next, and he could tell from Toby's posture that his lover was as well.

"But I was wrong," Gerard said. "Or perhaps the gentleman was, and he had approached this larger man in the hope of selling his services. The other man responded by punching him, hard, in the chest, and he fell backwards to the pavement."

Magnus's mouth opened but he didn't say anything.

"The big man left, and I hurried over to the man on the pavement to see if I could aid him. But I could tell immediately that he was dead. Though I did not know him by name then, I recognized the circumstances of his demise when I read about them in the paper."

He looked up at Magnus and Toby. "So you see, Mr. Walpert was killed before I arrived at your soirée."

"And what did you do then?" Toby asked.

"I ran away like a scared rabbit," Gerard said. "I knew there was nothing more I could do for him. And I was frightened that the big man might come back. I went directly to your home."

"This certainly adds a wrinkle to the story," Magnus said. "Could you identify that large man in court?"

Gerard shook his head. "I saw him only from behind. And Walpert was not a particularly tall man, so my impression could be altered by that."

Toby had another idea. "Do you bet on the fights?"

Gerard nodded. "Occasionally, though not to an extreme, and never more than I can afford to lose. Not like Walpert, though. He didn't have a farthing left when he left the arena. Or at least that's what he told me."

"Have you ever seen a large man at the arena accepting bets?" Toby asked.

Gerard shook his head. "If you want to place a bet, you signal a boy, who comes up to you and takes your money and gives you a chit. If you win, he returns to you, takes back the chit and hands over your winnings. If you lose, you can tear up the chit and walk away."

"So you never bet on credit?"

"I don't. But I have seen other men do so."

"Walpert?"

"I couldn't say. Though I recognized him that night, I'd never spoken to him before or taken special notice of him."

They finished their tea, and bid Gerard a good afternoon. "You won't bring my name into this, will you?" he asked nervously.

"Not without your express permission," Magnus said. "Though your testimony might be necessary to keep an innocent man from the gallows."

"And Richard Pemberton can rehearse your testimony with you, to remove all suspicion of inversion," Toby said. "You were simply a man at the fights who spoke to another. When you left the arena, you spotted the man you'd spoken with and witnessed the assault."

"No one could blame you for leaving once you established Walpert was dead," Magnus said. "I'd be frightened myself."

"Right now, we are at the very beginning of assembling pieces of a jigsaw puzzle," Toby said. "It is quite possible that we will be able to identify the assailant through other means."

They walked out to Bond Street and turned toward home. "What do you make of his story?" Magnus asked.

"I find it believable. My experience is not so wide as Gerard's, of course, but I have on occasion made eye contact with a man that was an expression of sexual interest."

"And have you pursued that?" Magnus asked.

Toby laughed. "Of course, my dear. I made no pretense of being a virgin before I met you. But since that morning in Gervase Quinn's office, I have had eyes for only you."

"I admit to more than my share of impulsive assignations," Magnus said. "Most of them at sea, though a few on land as well. But I never had the need to hand out coin afterwards."

"You are quite a bit more attractive than Gerard," Toby said. "And younger, to boot. Gerard is forty-five if a day, and though some men find a belly like his attractive, I'd find it difficult to secure a good purchase on his cock."

Magnus laughed deeply. "I didn't realize you had thought of him in that way."

"Magnus. I think of nearly every man I meet in that way. Don't you?"

"Honestly? Only the most attractive. And those I am curious about."

"Curious sounds a good deal like Curiel."

"And wouldn't you wish to wrap your hands around those muscles?" Magnus said. "I admit to some amount of jealousy of Silas, that he can explore that body. Curiel is a much more interesting lesson in anatomy than one could find in a book. Do you think the cock is a muscle?"

It was Toby's turn to laugh. "Keep your voice down, Magnus. We are in public. Did you not study anatomy at Eton?"

"Only in the most basic sense. I have no real idea of what goes on inside one." He leaned in close. "Though I do have a great understanding of the role of the cock and arse in generating pleasure."

"You dolt," Toby said, and elbowed him. "Do not forget the function of the prostate, which provides so much sexual pleasure in sodomy that it can lead to obsession."

"I do recall learning that male sexual excess leads to debility and female reproductive health is damaged by intellectual study," Magnus said.

The gray skies threatened to open at any minute, and Toby increased his pace until they approached Ormond Yard, so they could avoid being drenched. "We allowed ourselves to be distracted," Toby said as he slowed, once in view of their doorstep. "We have established that Gerard Houghton witnessed Nathan Walpert's murder, during a time when Silas and Ezra were at the Tabard Inn."

"And that is certainly a point to relay to Silas and Pemberton. But Gerard is reluctant to be involved, and can only identify the villain by his size."

The skies opened up as they reached the steps up to their door, and they managed to get inside with only a bit of dampness. "I don't know about you, but I could do with a whisky," Magnus said. "And then a solid supper, and some rejuvenating time upstairs."

"I am with you on all three counts," Toby said. "Though I do so with a care that poor Ezra is languishing in a gaol cell charged with murder, and it is upon those of us who know and care about him, and justice, to remove the shroud over him."

Chapter 21

Holding Cell

Ezra

"What are the charges against me?" Ezra demanded as the two bobbies escorted him out of the arena.

"You'll find out at Scotland Yard," one of them said.

But it was a lie. A pair of handcuffs was placed on his wrists. He was taken to Scotland Yard and placed in a temporary lock-up with a group of drunks, pickpockets, and other miscreants. At least there, the cuffs were removed from his wrists.

He tried to stay to himself, in a corner of the cell, but a drunk kept harassing him. "What you here for? Beat somebody up, you big lug?"

"If you aren't careful I'll do the same for you."

"Oh, a Frenchie, are you? Big mouth for a foreigner."

Ezra rose to his full height from the bench and flexed his arms. "If you know what's good for you you'll shut up and sit down."

The drunk stumbled backward. "All right, all right. Just making conversation."

He sat down again. Fortunately the bobbies had accompanied him into the locker room, so he was wearing street clothes instead of the shorts and singlet he wore into the ring. He pulled his cap down low on his head and shrunk into himself.

What had he done? He had been a good citizen. Except for his activities with Silas, he had broken no laws. And they'd kept their hands to themselves in public, only grappling with each other in private.

He'd been offered the chance to throw a match now and then, and always refused. And when he had the opportunity, he counseled other boxers to avoid such activities, providing the example of a man he had boxed against in Bristol who had been later discovered to be at the beck and call of a bookie. He had been banned from boxing after that, and forced to work as a stevedore.

Had one of the bookies taken his attitude against him and tried to get him out of the arena? Another boxer who was jealous of his skill and seeking to move up in the ranks? A dissatisfied bettor with a grudge against him?

Perhaps it all came down to his religion, as so many things did. Someone did not appreciate that a Hebrew, and a foreigner, could best native Englishmen, and wanted him out of the ring.

But until he knew what the charges were against him, he couldn't figure out why he had been arrested, or what he could do about it.

It was several hours before his name was called. Before he was released from the holding cell, a pair of cuffs was slapped on him again.

He was led to an interrogation room where a tall, cadaverous-looking man awaited him. "I am Detective Sergeant Collins," he said. "Have a seat."

He pointed to a wooden table with a seat on either side. "Can you take these off?" Ezra asked, holding up his cuffed hands.

Collins shook his head. "And let loose those bruising fists of yours? Not a chance."

"Why have you brought me here?" Ezra asked, as he sat. "I have done nothing wrong."

"Do you know a Mr. Nathan Walpert?"

At first Ezra was tempted to shake his head, but he thought for a moment. Walpert. Walpert? Why was that name familiar?

Finally he said, "I recognize it but cannot place it. The name sounds Hebrew to me. Does he attend the Bevis Marks synagogue in Aldgate?"

Collins nodded.

Ezra shrugged. "Then I might know him. Why is that important?"

Collins banged his fist on the table. "It is important because you slammed your fist into his belly last Friday night, hitting him so hard that he fell backwards against the paving stones."

"That is not true. I have never hit a man outside the boxing ring." In England, he added to himself. In France, as he was learning to defend himself, he had struck out many times, though almost always at boys of his own age, rather than men.

Collins ignored him. "Walpert hit his head so hard that he cracked his skull open and died almost instantly."

Ezra stared at him in open-eyed horror. "Why would I do such a thing?"

"That's exactly what we're here to find out," Collins said. "Why did you do it?"

"But I didn't."

For the next hour, Ezra denied knowing Walpert beyond a possible connection through the synagogue. He denied hitting the man. "What reason would I have to hit a stranger?"

Finally Collins gave up. "If you will not cooperate, Mr. Curiel, then I have little choice but to send you back to your cell to await a judgment before the grand jury."

"What about bail?" Ezra asked. "My wife can raise the necessary funds."

"That is highly unlikely, as it is her evidence that has led us to arrest you," Collins said drily. "In any event, murder is an indictable offense. The question of bail cannot be considered until after the grand jury examines the evidence against you. They will issue an indictment and indicate whether you should be allowed bail."

Ezra was reeling from the idea that Rebecca could have provided evidence against him. What kind of evidence? How?

"You are still a French citizen, aren't you?" Collins asked.

"I still hold a French passport, yes, but I consider myself a resident of London now."

"The court will take that into account in deciding to approve bail."

Collins stepped up to the door and opened it. "You can take him back to the cell now," he said to an officer in the hallway.

Ezra rose and was taken back to the same holding cell. Throughout the night, men were brought in and out of the cell. Some returned; others did not.

He despaired of ever leaving the fetid cell. The food was terrible and he could barely drink the water. All the men had to use the same pot to piss and shit. Collins never called him back and there was nothing he could do but try to sleep.

Then on Saturday morning, his name was called again. A gaoler took him into another interview room. "You had some money when we brought you in," he said. "As you're going to be in police custody for a while, you have the opportunity to transfer to the Queen's Bench prison in Southwark."

"What does that mean?"

"Eight of the better cells are set aside for those who can afford them. Half-a-crown a-week to rent one of those. At the end of the prison is a kind of market, consisting of several sheds, occupied by butchers, poulterers, green-grocers. So you can buy yourself your own food, not the slop we serve here."

"I'll do it," Ezra said. "Where do I sign?"

"No signing necessary. I'll arrange for your transport. Course there's a fee for that."

"You can take it out of the money of mine you're holding. And take an extra shilling for your trouble."

"With pleasure," the gaoler said.

The accommodations at the Queen's Bench were certainly better than the holding cells where he'd been. He had a room to himself, large enough so that he could exercise. But even so, he remembered that he was a prisoner, and he didn't know how he could ever be released. Eventually his money would run out, or he'd be convicted, and he'd be locked up for the rest of his days.

Chapter 22

Case Law

Silas

Silas forced himself to wait until a civilized hour on Sunday morning to call at Wigton's flat. He was desperate to know if the solicitor had been able to speak with Ezra, and gain his representation. As well as to know anything else Wigton had been able to discover.

"Come in, Silas," Wigton said, answering the door himself. "I expected you to show up today."

"Did you speak with Ezra?"

"I did." Wigton led him into the lounge, which was free of undergarments and beer glasses. "I located him in the Queen's Bench prison in Southwark. Because he had a significant sum of cash with him when arrested, he had already been able to establish himself in one of the state rooms, which is fortunate."

"What are those?"

"One of the rooms in the prison set apart for the better class of prisoners."

Silas was relieved. He had imagined Ezra in a dank, windowless cell, deprived of all but a cup of water and a crust of bread.

Wigton continued, "He insists he is innocent, and when I told him that you were willing to offer him an alibi, he confirmed all the details you had given me. Independently, of course. But your stories match in almost every detail, which is good."

"Were you able to get him released?"

Wigton shook his head. "He will appear before a magistrate tomorrow morning to answer to the charges against him. At that time, Richard Pemberton will stand to represent him. According to Mr. Curiel he owns the house in Hackney where he lives with his wife, and can offer that as surety so that he can be released while waiting for trial."

"That's excellent," Silas said. "And I have recruited friends to help discover evidence that could support Ezra's case."

He outlined the assignments that Pemberton had given each of them the day before.

"This is all very good," Wigton said. "You'll ensure that Pemberton is at the court tomorrow at the appointed time?"

"I will," Silas said. They talked for a few more minutes, and Silas felt some of his anxiety draining away. Ezra was in a very serious situation, and there were risks to anyone who stood up in his defense, but Silas had faith in the machinery of the court that the truth would come out. He knew it was naïve, and he had seen several instances where innocent men went to prison, but those men had all been guilty of other crimes, so there was some justice. Ezra was innocent of this charge, he was sure.

He left Wigton's apartment. He was desperate to talk to his friends, but they all had their individual assignments, and he still had more to do. He walked down Oxford Street where the businesses had already opened, and ladies looked in shop windows and conferred with friends about the latest styles in bonnets and gloves. Where once he would have been jealous of those with money to spend, now he thought them frivolous. A man's life hung in the balance! What was a new top hat to him?

He entered Holbom, and the tall trees and hidden corners of Lincoln's Inn Fields beckoned to him. He often strolled over there if he had a few spare minutes to eat his lunch or simply to think, but now he hurried forward to the office at the Inns of Court and let himself in. The buildings were quiet, and he moved his desk closer to the window to sit in the light, and began to look through the law books that lined Pemberton's office.

The barrister had charged him with finding similar cases, where one person's actions had inadvertently led to another's death. Some of the cases he found involved liability. In one, a boat owner had not taken care to ensure his vessel was seaworthy. When it sank in the Thames, he had been charged with the deaths of several passengers.

That wasn't quite the issue here, but Silas still took notes on it. In another case, two men had been fighting outside a bar over one man's advances toward the other's wife. Both had sustained serious injuries, resulting in the death of one man. In that case, Silas felt, both were at fault, and the decision revolved around who had started the fight.

And so it went, book after book, case after case. The best he could come up with was a defense against involuntary manslaughter. According to the law, such a crime occurred when the accused did not intend to cause death or serious injury but caused the death of another through recklessness or criminal negligence.

As he made note of that, he was surprised by the appearance of Richard Pemberton at the office. "I see you're hard at work, Silas," Pemberton said, as he took off his coat. "What have you found so far?"

"I spoke with Mr. Wigton earlier, and he has agreed to take on Ezra's case. I have added the time of the hearing tomorrow morning to your calendar."

"Very good."

"As you suggested, while my friends research other motives and suspects in Walpert's murder, I turned to how you might construct a defense, if the case were to come to trial. It seems that given the circumstances the charge might be reduced to involuntary manslaughter. Is that your assumption as well?"

"It is. But involuntary manslaughter has two components."

"Recklessness and criminal negligence," Silas said.

"Very good. What is the definition of recklessness, then?"

Silas flipped through his notes. "Suppose a man called John dropped a brick off a bridge, and the brick landed on the head of another man, Sebastian, killing him."

Pemberton nodded. "Go on."

"If John merely intended to drop the brick, not to kill anyone, then he would not be guilty of recklessness. But if he knew that people were walking beneath him, and there was a chance that his brick could his someone, then dropping the brick would be a reckless act."

"Exactly. The *mens rea*, or knowledge of wrongdoing, required for murder does not exist in that case."

"How would that apply to Ezra?"

"It is difficult to speculate because we are operating on the assumption that Mr. Curiel was not the assailant. But picking up on your example, let's say this man John hit Mr. Walpert. John is an ordinary man, not a boxer or someone who has undergone training. He hits Mr. Walpert in anger, unaware that he could cause significant damage to Mr. Walpert's person or cause his death. Then his attack on Mr. Walpert could be a reckless act and considered 'constructive' manslaughter.' The penalty for such a crime would be significantly less than if there is criminal intent."

Silas hurriedly scribbled down what Pemberton said, knowing that he would have to go back and recopy the writing more clearly.

"How would the state prove criminal intent?" Silas asked.

"As a trained boxer, Mr. Curiel is presumed to understand his own strength, as well as in what ways he can punch or hit an opponent without causing serious injury. If he ignored that understanding in his attack on Mr. Walpert, then the crime would be judged much more serious."

Silas nodded, and took more notes. "I will need examples of cases that operated under each circumstance," he said.

"I'll keep reading and researching."

"Good lad." Pemberton had some work of his own to do, and he stayed in the office for an hour. Silas read and took notes all afternoon, until the light began to die and his eyes were tired and his hand sore. Finally he walked home at dusk. Had he done enough that day to help Ezra?

And why did it matter so much to him? That was the greatest puzzle of all. He had learned through painful experience that he could not rely on a lover for much more than a quick roll in the sheets or a wild suck in an alley. Ezra had shown him so much more, accepting Silas's faults, his flightiness, his love of color and sensual fabric. He risked his livelihood, his marriage, and his reputation to keep coming to Silas's bed.

Was it just that Silas worshipped his muscles? He had never before been with a man who was so – manly, if he had to use a word. A man who was strong enough to lift him up, to hold him in the air while spearing him from below. Nor had he been with someone who whispered such endearments, and who appeared genuinely pleased simply to see him.

Was that enough to keep them together? What would happen if Ezra was found guilty, or had to flee the country? What would Silas do then?

Chapter 23

A Smoke

John

"What is on your agenda, or Janner's?" Raoul asked John, as they lay together in bed on Sunday morning.

"I will devote today to helping Silas," John said. "I will head to New Cross and speak to the locals about the boxing ring, and if it is dangerous to be around there at night. It is possible that Mr. Walpert's death was at the hands of a thief who was angered that Walpert had nothing to steal."

"Is there anything I can do to help you?" Raoul asked.

"I could use your language skills," John said. "Especially if I run across any Frenchmen or Germans."

"I should look French, but common," Raoul said. "I can manage that. I still have some clothes I wore at university."

John smiled. "So fine living hasn't expanded your waistline since then?"

"I did little enough fine living until I met you. And my university clothes were hand-me-downs from Father Maurice, so they were baggy even then."

After a quick breakfast, they dressed without Beller's help, as he regularly took Sundays off to visit his family. And, John suspected, court a young lady whom he had met through the offices of his sister. If Beller proposed, he would have to inform her of the character of the home where he served, and ensure she was agreeable to join their household. If she wasn't, then Beller would have to choose between her and his position.

The position wasn't much, John admitted as he and Raoul walked out. Raoul had grudgingly accepted Beller's help in maintaining his wardrobe, and Beller and Jane, the housemaid, kept the home clean. Beller helped John with his broadsides by asking questions of his acquaintances and running errands.

If Beller were to marry, his wife would take over the maid's duties, and perhaps some of the cooking. John and Raoul were both out all day during the week, John on his research and Raoul at his office. They dined out most nights, at parties or at the local chophouse. By virtue of his title, John was welcome anywhere that Raoul was invited to represent the French embassy. Hostesses were always glad to have an extra man on hand, especially one who held a title and could dance.

Someday, his father would die, and John would inherit the Earl's title and Briar House on Eaton Square. Beller would become the butler and his wife the housekeeper, and there would be footmen and maids and perhaps even separate valets for him and Raoul. He would have to entertain as well as provide a city residence for his sisters, if they chose to visit.

It was all too much to contemplate, he thought. They walked outside and he hailed a carriage, which passed by without a second look. Then he remembered how they were dressed. He took off his flat cap and straightened his shoulders, assuming an air of lordship even though his coat was shabby. Another carriage passed them by, but the third pulled to a stop.

"Deptford Green," he told the carriage driver, and handed him a coin.

He and Raoul climbed inside. "Is that address near the boxing hall?" Raoul asked.

"A few blocks away. An easy landmark to head for, and I never like to alight from a carriage in the immediate vicinity where I intend to conduct my enquiries." He pulled the flat cap from his pocket and affected a lower-class accent. "Don't want anyone to think I'm a toff."

Raoul laughed. "You are the best at concealing your true self of anyone I have ever met. Even Father Maurice, who hid his desires from his congregation, could not keep up the farce to me."

"It is a skill I learned early," John said, as the carriage racketed over the cobblestones. "Both at home and at school. It was too dangerous to let anyone know the real me."

"I learned similar skills of deception from Father Maurice," Raoul said. "It has been hard for me to shed those habits. Only with you do I feel I can really be myself."

"It must be very difficult for Silas's lover," John said. "To be in such a masculine profession, constantly in contact with other men's bodies, and yet hold back."

"And outside the ring, he has a wife," Raoul said. "Imagine the deception necessary there."

"We don't know if he performs with her as he does with Silas," John said. "Many men do. And they are content with the bifurcated nature of their existence."

"Able to match their desires to the one they are with," Raoul said. "It still seems awkward to me."

The carriage reached their destination and John gave the driver an extra farthing for his trouble. It was a Sunday morning, so many of those they passed on the street were in their church-going clothes and not to be disrupted. Raoul heard his native language coming from a group of men smoking cigarettes in front of a barber shop, and he left John to speak with them.

John aimed for an older man sitting on a bench at the edge of the green, in view of the boxing arena. "Know what time the fights start?" he asked, as he sat down.

"Only practice today," the man said. "Ain't right to box on the

Lord's holy day." Then he laughed. "Not like you'd find any holy men there any day of the week."

John pulled a paper packet of cigarettes and a box of matches from his pocket, and offered a smoke to the stranger. "Don't mind if I do," the man said.

John struck a match and lit the man's cigarette and his own. He didn't smoke, as a habit, but found it a useful way to insinuate himself with a stranger he wanted to speak to.

"You get over there any?" John asked. "I'm John, by the way."

"Eddy. And thank ye for the smoke." He inhaled deeply. "I like watching the boxing of an evening, but you wouldn't catch me betting."

"Really? Why not? Are the matches fixed?"

"Sometimes." Eddy took a deep drag on his cigarette. "You get a real good fighter, like Big Mo, that African man, and you know you can't bet against him. Nobody hardly does except the fools."

"What about that Jew—the Hammering Hebrew, they call him."

"Ah, he's a smart one. Ye've only to watch him on his feet to see he knows what he's about. Naw, the ones ye know the name of, they're fighting on the square. It's when they put up two local lads that men can win or lose money. Those are the ones I think are fixed."

"I'll keep that in mind," John said. "What about the neighborhood? Is it safe to walk around at night? I heard a man was murdered there a while ago."

"It's dicey, I'll give ye that," Eddy said. "If I'm out and about I like to stay to the main streets. Course, I don't look like I'm worth the trouble to rob from. But they get up to odd things in those alleys. Men with men, if ye know what I mean."

"I'll steer clear, then," John said. He finished his cigarette, bid good-day to Eddy, and continued toward the boxing arena.

Raoul joined him on the way. "I could not find any Frenchman who might be able to give me information, but I did encounter a rather shifty-eyed man who tried to entice me into an alley where he could service me."

"You didn't accept, did you?"

Raoul shook his head. "You are quite enough for me to handle, mon cher. But I heard some German in his accent, and I told him I'd give him a coin if he'd talk to me for a few minutes."

"And did he have anything interesting to say?"

"He didn't know anything about boxing, but he did say that he knew Nathan Walpert when they were both boys."

"Really?"

"They attended the same Ragged School for a while. But Walpert was smart and found a way out, while the fellow I spoke with didn't have the same head for numbers or writing. He left the school and began to make his way the only way he could, with his mouth and arse."

"That is sad," John said. "I wish there was more we could do for these boys."

"This fellow might have started out as a boy, but he was a full-grown man," Raoul said. "He did say that when they were boys, he had tried to convince young Nathan to pick up a few extra coins with him, and Nathan was torn. He might easily have ended up in the same situation if it wasn't for his schoolmaster."

They followed their instincts for the rest of the morning and then the early afternoon. In separate conversations, they learned more about the dangerous nature of the streets around the boxing arena, where men who were big winners might be followed into the darkness. A regular bettor said that the man who controlled the numbers was called Bertie Greenbaum, and they also heard the name Alfie Gibbons, who might work for Greenbaum or might be another bookie. It wasn't clear.

Their ramblings eventually took them to the Thames, where they had a rare view of the Cutty Sark, the clipper ship that was at the height of the tea trade, making its way down the river toward the Channel, and then the Orient.

"Magnificent, isn't she?" John asked. "They say she cost over sixteen thousand pounds to build, can reach Shanghai in three and a half months, and can carry a million pounds of tea."

"Yes, quite a marvel," Raoul said. "We French have nothing to compare to her."

He sniffed John's breath. "You have smoked quite a lot today. You must wash your mouth out when we return home if you have hope for any kisses this evening."

"No reward for all I have learned?" John said in mock dismay.

"Oh, there will be a reward," Raoul said. "But only under my conditions."

"Harsh taskmaster," John said. He stuffed his flat cap back in his pocket and set out to gain a carriage to take them home. He would pass on what he learned to the others on Monday.

Chapter 24

National Security

Toby

Toby left early on Monday morning for the Foreign Office, hoping to catch Gervase Quinn for a few minutes before he got too busy. The first post had already arrived, but it had nothing of specific import so he left it on the hall table, and then spotted their postman continuing the first round of deliveries to Ormond Yard.

On his way, he passed several delivery boys in horse and cart or and even one on a newfangled bicycle. The streets were littered with horse dung, and he crossed several times to avoid the most pungent smells.

His name was already known to the young man at the front desk who controlled entry and exit, so he passed quickly through the main hall and took the stairs to Quinn's office. The door was open, so he rapped lightly on the frame.

Quinn looked up from his paperwork. "Good morning, Marsh. We didn't have an appointment, did we?"

"No. I was hoping to take five minutes of your time."

"Come in, then. All this dratted paper will wait. Have you learned something that might be of interest to us?"

Part of the connection between Toby, Magnus and the Foreign Office was that they would keep their ears open for anything that might affect her majesty's government. "I'm honestly not sure," Toby said as he sat. "I have come into possession of some information about the death of Mr. Nathan Walpert."

"Now you have my attention," Quinn said. "He has been the subject of much conversation here. Officers have been despatched to Walpert's office to review what he knew about this Suez deal and whether that information might have been compromised."

"You know, of course, that the soirées Magnus and I host attract a certain kind of men," Toby said.

"Would that include Mr. Walpert?"

Toby shook his head. "Neither of us has any knowledge of him."

Quinn knitted his hands together in front of him. "Then you must be referring to his alleged assailant, Mr. Curiel."

"As you can imagine that knowledge is very delicate, and could potentially ruin the career of an innocent man."

"You are certain of his innocence?"

"Reasonably certain. He has entered into a connection with a friend of ours, Silas Warner, a law clerk for barrister Richard Pemberton. According to Silas, Mr. Curiel fought in an early bout, and then the two of them decamped from the boxing arena to dine together at the Tabard Inn. From there, they attended a soirée at our home."

"Interesting."

"Magnus and I have gone over the timetable with Silas, and with another guest who would prefer to remain nameless at this time. Our guest states that at the time Silas and Ezra were at dinner, he was at the fights. He happened to find himself leaving the arena shortly after Mr. Walpert."

"For an assignation?"

"If there was one intended, it was only on the part of our guest, not Walpert. Our guest witnessed a conversation between Walpert and a much larger man, which resulted in the large man punching Walpert in the chest. Walpert fell to the ground and the assailant departed. Our guest, whose father was a physician, is acquainted with the signs of death. He hurried over to Walpert, quickly identified that he was dead, and left."

"Your guest, as you call him, must immediately report to the police," Quinn said.

"It's not that easy," Toby said. "First, he cannot identify the assailant as he only saw him from behind, in the dark. Second, he does not want to admit to attending our soirée."

"Your guest didn't overhear anything of the conversation between the two men?"

"Not as far as he has told us. He was not close to them, and there was a great deal of noise from the ongoing fight."

"So we have no way of knowing if this assault was related to Walpert's work."

"Both Silas and our guest have indicated that Walpert was a gambling man, and both have suspected that he might have met with someone from his bookmaker's."

"Since you have shared some confidence with me, I will share some in return," Quinn said. "It is our understanding that Walpert was indeed a gambler, and that he might have been in significant debt. It is feared that he might have passed compromising documents in exchange for the release of that debt. However your evidence casts doubt on that."

Quinn frowned. "Do you think Walpert's death was an accident?"

Toby nodded. "From our guest's testimony to us. And if he was a gambler, it makes no sense to kill him while he owes a significant debt."

"That is certainly true. It is a complicated scenario. Any ideas why Curiel's wife would put him in the frame if he is innocent?"

"It's possible that she knows about his dalliance with our friend Silas. Putting him in gaol would free her to administer his funds and operate as an independent woman."

"The fair sex. They often have schemes against us, don't they?

Sometimes I envy you, Marsh. You and Magnus have found a way to live that does not require a female." Then he smiled. "Though I must admit the ladies have attributes that balance out their troubles."

"Is the Foreign Office taking further steps to investigate Mr. Walpert's death?" Toby asked.

"In conjunction with Scotland Yard, of course," Quinn said. "I believe a detective will be interviewing Mr. Curiel, or already has, about his connections to Walpert and any knowledge of the Suez deal."

"We will keep you informed of anything relevant we find," Toby said.

"And consider convincing your guest to speak with the police," Quinn said. "From what you have told me, his evidence could be useful, and what he did after seeing Mr. Walpert die is not relevant."

He stood. "And then I must say goodbye, as I have a great deal of paperwork to go through, and I want to reserve some time to consider what you have told me. Be aware, though, that Walpert's death is potentially a case of national security, which will increase the pressure on both the legal system and Scotland Yard to bring this case to a quick conclusion."

Chapter 25

Queen's Bench

Silas

Monday morning, Silas reviewed the work that had to be done that week, and instructed Luke, the new junior clerk, in as much of it as he could before he accompanied Pemberton to Ezra's hearing before the Queen's Bench, which had jurisdiction over criminal cases such as murder. "Usually a case of this stature would be heard under the chief justice, but he is ailing," Pemberton said, as they walked out of the Inns of Court. "So we have been assigned to Justice Kenyon, one of the puisne judges."

"Puny?" Silas asked.

Pemberton spelled it. "It's an outdated French term for an ordinary judge. As you are exposed to more of the court system, you'll find that we have retained many terms from French or Old English."

They entered Palace Yard, and Pemberton nodded to a few of the white-wigged gownsmen who straggled into the huge hall, followed here and there by an ink-stained clerk like Silas or an anxious client.

Pemberton led the way to the lobby of the Queen's Bench Court, where an old woman sat at an apple-stall, selling a collection of gingerbread and sweet-stuff, and close by the side of a roaring fire large enough to roast a baron of beef.

Silas was in awe of everything. He followed Pemberton through a set of tall curtains and into a single chamber, some forty feet square, and about that many feet in height as well. It was a gloomy, wintry day, and the room was only dimly lit from a domed circular lantern in the roof. Pemberton moved easily through the crowd in his gown and wig, and Silas struggled to keep up with him.

The judge sat under a carved canopy in front of the royal arms, on a dais. Silas could only imagine how it must feel to be a defendant in such a court. And what of years or decades earlier when the actual sovereign would sit in judgment?

Judge Kenyon sported a white wig like Pemberton's, but with two large side appendages that rested upon his shoulders. He wore a large scarlet gown with many folds, all of it brocaded with ermine.

Pemberton motioned Silas to a seat in the pit, amongst other clerks, witnesses, and anyone who had business before the court. He took his own place at a long table which had been amply supplied with writing materials.

Silas sat quietly as other cases were brought up and quickly despatched. It was clear that Kenyon had no patience for fools, and the smartest barristers, like Pemberton, kept their discourse to a minimum. When Ezra's case was called, Pemberton stood and addressed the judge. "Mr. Curiel is a well-known figure in the community and owns a home in Hackney which he can supply as a surety to allow him release from prison until his trial."

That was all, Silas wondered? No attempt to lay out the case against Ezra and rebut its charges? But Pemberton knew what he was doing. Judge Kenyon agreed to bail, slapped his gavel, and moved on.

Pemberton then rose and left the table, motioning for Silas to follow him. "Is that all?" Silas asked, when they were back in the lobby with the old woman.

"All we have to do," Pemberton said. "Wigton will arrange the bail and have Mr. Curiel released. Please go to Ormond Yard now and confirm that we will be able to have a meeting there this evening to discuss strategy. Take a carriage there and collect the fare from the office account, because time is of the essence."

Silas nodded.

Pemberton continued, "If that is acceptable, send invitations to Mr. Desjardins and Lord Therkenwell, and then compose a note requesting Mr. Curiel join us and have Robb carry it to the prison. I would rather that Mrs. Curiel not be aware of what we are doing, because we don't know her motives in this case."

Pemberton stopped to talk to another barrister, and Silas hurried out to the Strand, where he flagged down a carriage. When they reached Ormond Yard, he had the carriage wait until he was able to confirm, via Will and then Magnus, that the group could meet there that evening.

He sat back in the carriage for the return to the Inns of Court. He felt quite above his station scurrying around the city by carriage where he was accustomed to walking, and wondered if that would be a part of his new job replacing Cyril. Though if he recalled, Cyril had stayed glued to his desk and sent Silas out on his errands.

When he returned to the office he wrote invitations to John and Raoul, and the note to Ezra. "Take this to Mr. Curiel at Southwark Prison," he said to Robb. "If you have already missed him, then go to the bailiff's office, or failing that to his address in Hackney. Take care not to hand it to Mrs. Curiel. Then deliver the other two, which are of lesser importance."

Robb agreed and took off. Luke had some questions about a document he was copying, and Silas looked it over with him. He was pleased to see that the new boy had a good handwriting and an attention to detail. They talked through the problems and Silas returned to the other cases on his desk. An hour or more later, Robb returned, having hand-delivered the message to Ezra. "He read it and said he will be there," he said. "I also left the notes you wrote at Eaton Square and the French Consulate."

"Excellent. Now I have these documents which must be delivered to Wigton's office."

"Will he be given an invitation this evening as well?" Robb asked. "Because I could take that at the same time."

Pemberton had returned from court by then, so Silas stuck his head in the door of the office and asked. "Come inside, please, and shut the door," Pemberton said.

Silas was worried. Had he done or said something that morning to cause offense?

"The meeting this evening will be populated largely by inverts," Pemberton said. "Since Wigton is not one of us, I would rather we not involve him directly. I will control what information he receives."

"Very good, sir," Silas said, and returned to the outer office where he told Robb not to mention the dinner to Wigton or anyone in his office.

He went back to work, but his thoughts were consumed by the late Nathan Walpert. He was a very average-looking man, like many of the middle-class men who crowded the hall, and nothing about him spoke out, either as a consummate gambler or an invert.

The life of men like him was always shadowed by violence. Make a move to the wrong man, and you could be reported to the police, beaten, or even killed. He had heard several cases of men near molly houses or in lonely alleys who had approached the wrong man for sex.

Was that the cause of Walpert's death? And if he was killed for being a man who loved men, what did that mean for Silas? If he was on his own once again, would he have to be wary of every man who caught his eye?

Chapter 26

Root of All Evil

Magnus

Monday morning, after Toby had left for the Foreign Office, Magnus sat down with Will in the lounge to compose a list of all those who he recalled had been present at the soirée the night Nathan Walpert was murdered. It was difficult, because nearly two weeks had passed, and during that evening many men, and some women, had come in and out, occasionally as guests of someone who had been invited.

"I'm fairly certain Sir Arthur Sullivan was there," Magnus said. "Because I recall seeing him at the fencing yard and he was most keen to join us."

"His name is here on the list of those invited," Will said.

Will had never been educated beyond the second grade, and during his time as a houseboy for Magnus's father, the late duke, nothing had been done to improve that. Since coming to work for Magnus, though, both Carlo and Will spent time each day practicing their letters. It was important that Will be able to read invoices and calculate sums, and for Carlo to be able to read recipes and figure out what ingredients and in what quantities were necessary.

"This man here, Mr. Rosetti," Will said. "He was here with a woman, wasn't he?"

"Yes, he was. He's a painter. The woman with him was his sister, Christina, a writer. While they are of the artistic tendency, and not always believed by the courts, we might rely on them simply to testify that they saw Ezra here. If indeed they did."

Toby returned later that morning and told Magnus what he had learned from Gervase Quinn. "This works in our favor," he said. "If Quinn is concerned about the political implications of Walpert's death, it gives us some leave to investigate ourselves, on his implied behalf."

"It will be interesting to see what Raoul has learned at the embassy," Magnus said. "Things are moving ahead quickly. I am glad Pemberton asked us to arrange a dinner this evening for our cohort."

Toby stood. "Yes, I need to confer with Carlo on the menu. And you might want to bring in some more wine—I noticed we were running low when everyone was here on Saturday."

While Toby spoke with Carlo, Magnus conferred with Will, and they created a list. "Shall I go out to Hambly's?" Will asked. They bought the bulk of their wine from that shop.

"No, I need to go to Steingrob's," Magnus said. That was a shop that John had recommended to them, where they sold a Riesling that Magnus was fond of.

"Steingrob is a Jew, and he may know of Ezra's family, and be able to give us some insight into why Mrs. Curiel was willing to testify against her husband."

Magnus pulled on a heavy overcoat and strode out to Regent Square and Samuel Steingrob's shop. A brisk breeze pushed the soot in the air away, allowing a bleak sun to shine. He walked the few blocks to Steingrob's shop his mind focused not only on wine, but on what he might ask the old Jew.

"Good afternoon, my lord," Steingrob said, with an accent redolent of Eastern Europe. He was an elderly man with a white beard and a skullcap, and an encyclopedic knowledge of wine.

He offered Magnus a taste of a new vintage of red wine that had come in from Burgundy, and knowing that Raoul came from that area, Magnus ordered a case. He ordered a case of Chardonnay as well as one case of his favorite Riesling. While they roamed the store and he tasted several different wines, Magnus thought about how to bring up the subject of Ezra Curiel. To call him a friend would attach a label to him—he was sure that Steingrob knew about his household with Toby.

"A man who has come to our soirées in the past has been in the news of late," Magnus finally said. "I believe he would be a countryman of yours. Ezra Curiel."

"He is a Jew, yes, but with his nose in the air," Steingrob said. "The Spaniards disdain those of us who carry our religion in our faces and our clothing."

"Is that so? But not very remarkable," Magnus said. "My mother does not care for our nearest neighbor in Cornwall because though she is a very pretty woman with elegant manners and is the wife of a wealthy landowner, her father was a farmer."

"There are good and bad in every community," Steingrob said. "There are men who come to my shul, and are ostentatious in their prayer, who I would not wish to meet in a dark alley."

"Really? Of what sort are they?"

"Bookmakers, gamblers, brothel owners," Steingrob said.

Magnus opened his mouth, but had nothing to say.

"You are surprised, my lord," Steingrob said. "One of my best customers owns a brothel in Aldgate that offers our young women to many who would not otherwise speak to a Jew. Yes, these young women are beautiful, but to an Englishman they are also exotic. I do not approve of that trade, but I have to make a living. So I shut my eyes and hold my nose."

He shook his head. "The bookmakers are even worse. They know they can ruin people with their greed, but they do it anyway. Some even prey exclusively on our countrymen—and women."

"Women gamblers?"

"Yes, some women can have the same venal desires as men. More excitement, more money. Though in their cases, the bookmaker comes to their homes, rather than meeting them at the races or the arena."

"It must be a scandal to your people."

Steingrob shrugged. "I cannot live any man's life other than my own."

"The man Mr. Curiel is accused of murdering was another Jew, Nathan Walpert. Did you know him?"

"Only from the shul. He said he did not have much of a taste for wine. But I believe his money was going to the bookmaker, Greenbaum."

The bell on the door rang, and another customer entered. Magnus arranged to have the wine charged to his account and delivered to the house that afternoon, and returned to Ormond Yard, considering what Steingrob had told him.

He didn't have a chance to discuss anything with Toby, though, because soon after he got home, Will brought Sylvia Cooke and Jess Cleaver into the parlor. "We have been out visiting," Sylvia said, as she handed her cloak to Will. "We dropped in on Mrs. Curiel to pay our respects."

Jess handed over her coat and scarf as well, and the ladies sat. "She did not appear to be a woman in mourning for the state of her husband," Jess said. "If anything, her behavior was somewhat festive."

"Festive?" Magnus asked.

"She wore a pale pink gown that did not suit her coloring, with a large bow at the shoulder," Sylvia said.

Carlo brought in the silver teapot that Magnus's mother had gifted him, originally from the family's country house, on a matching silver tray with sugar and creamer. Will followed him with a tray of cups, saucers, small plates, and freshly baked crumpets. The crumpets were light and spongy and served with lemon curd.

"And you found this attire unseemly in a woman whose husband faces the charge of murder?" Toby asked.

"It wasn't that I expected to see her in dark clothing, her garments rent with worry," Sylvia said. "But she was quite cheerful in welcoming us, as if we had come to a party."

"She offered us a Victoria sponge with strawberry jam!" Jess said. "There were three other women there, obviously her close confidantes, and they all seemed to be celebrating something."

"That is curious," Magnus said.

"There was one other odd thing," Sylvia said. "One of the other women said something to Mrs. Curiel when she thought I wouldn't hear."

"Sylvia has the senses of an owl," Magnus said. "I swear she can see in the dark and hear the movements of a mouse."

"Thank you for that flattering description," Sylvia said drily. "The other woman said something like 'at least you shall be free of that awful Mr. Greenbaum.' Does that name mean anything to you?"

Toby shook his head, but Magnus said, "Samuel Steingrob, the wine merchant, mentioned that name to me as well. He implied that man is a bookmaker who preyed particularly on the Jewish community."

"While Sylvia was speaking with Mrs. Curiel, I had an interesting conversation with one of the other women, a Mrs. Mendoza," Jess said. "Apparently there is some friction between elements of the Jewish community."

"How so?" Magnus asked.

"There are families like the Curiels and the Mendozas, who have their roots in Spain and France," Jess said. "From what I gather, they arrived in Britain with money, and have strived to associate with the higher classes. Then there are the newer immigrants from Germany and Russia, who have rougher manners and are more likely to work as peddlers. I imagine this Mr. Greenbaum would fall into that category."

"Mrs. Curiel's husband works with his fists," Toby said. "That should not entitle her to any special regard."

Jess nodded. "Indeed. And Mrs. Mendoza implied that Mrs.

Curiel might be able to rise in society if she shed her husband, and perhaps married another with greater wealth and influence. Though she is not an attractive woman, she has a certain flair to her. What the French would call a *jolie laide*. A woman of unusual, flawed, or quirky looks."

Toby retrieved his notebook from the office and had Jess spell the names they had learned that day. "Greenbaum would be a name of German origin," he said. "So one of the newer immigrants. Perhaps he has tried to sell the Curiels something, or insinuate himself with Ezra."

"Or he makes book on Ezra's fights," Magnus said. "I wonder if Ezra has ever colluded with him in the past."

"You believe he would throw a match?" Toby asked.

"I don't know. He is very proud of his physique, and his prowess, and to deliberately lose a match would probably hurt his pride. But we are talking about money here."

"Timothy 6:10 says that money is the root of all evil," Jess said. "And though the Jews do not read that portion of the Bible, I am sure that affects them as well as those of us who do—or profess to."

Chapter 27

Embassy Buzz

Raoul

On Monday morning at the French embassy, Raoul didn't have to bring up the topic of the Suez Canal deal and the implications of Nathan Walpert's murder. It was all that anyone wanted to talk about, and his colleagues, and even those from other departments, wanted to hear his opinion.

He arrived early, as was his practice. He thought it set a good standard for the men who had previously been his colleagues, and now worked under him. He had inherited a small office with a richly patterned Oriental carpet and floral wall coverings, which was too fussy for his taste. But he was reluctant to ask for changes for fear that his own supervisors would think him arrogant.

He opened the heavy damask drape over the window that looked out over Knightsbridge. The winter sun was weak, the trees across from him denuded of their leaves. He settled in the leather-upholstered chair behind his large mahogany desk and arranged the papers he had carried home with him: contracts he had reviewed and missives from Paris. He liked his desk to be neat and well-organized.

The bookcase along one wall was lined with leather-bound volumes in French and English—trade regulations and other laws, for the most part, as well as several atlases and dictionaries of foreign languages. He had placed several mementos of his life in France there, including a tiny wooden wine barrel to remind him of the vineyards where his father worked.

His staff filtered in, taking their desks in the high-ceilinged room outside his office. Each desk had a small gas lamp to supplement the recently-installed electric lighting. A painting of Adolphe Thiers, the first President of the French Third Republic, hung on the rear wall, as if to oversee their work.

Each morning at ten o'clock, a waitress in a uniform pushed a tea cart through the office, providing coffee or tea and small pastries to those who wished to partake. Raoul stepped out of his office and took a cup and saucer, as well as a plate with two madeleines, over to the desk where his colleague Alexandre worked. He had the most direct contact with bankers.

"What is the news this morning?" he asked.

"Everyone I spoke with is frightened," Alexandre said. He had already gotten his coffee, though he had taken two shortbread biscuits with his.

"Frightened of what?"

"Did you not hear? Nathan Walpert was murdered!"

Though Raoul knew exactly who Walpert was, he wanted to know what Alexandre knew. "Who was he?"

Alexandre shook his head. "You are the head of this department. You should be aware of all these things. Walpert was one of the bankers involved in the deal for Britain to acquire shares in the Suez Canal."

Raoul leaned against Alexandre's mahogany desk, which was smaller and less ornate than his own. Such small details made a bureaucracy work, he thought.

"I certainly know about that. But why would someone murder a banker?"

Alexandre lowered his voice. "That is what everyone is talking about at Rothschild's," he said. "Did Walpert know something? Was he in collusion with some partner to the deal?"

Raoul said nothing, just nodded.

"And those on the other floors of this building are worried about repercussions from the British. That perhaps there might be an uproar of anti-French sentiment that would put us all at risk."

Their other colleague Gabriel joined the conversation, carrying his own coffee cup. "The rumor among bankers is that Walpert was heavily in debt."

"How did you hear that?" Raoul asked. Behind him he saw Gabriel's desk, cluttered with papers, quills and ink, as well as no fewer than three open books.

"I had a drink last week after work with Hugo Malherbe," Gabriel said. He looked studiously down at his coffee, as if he was afraid it would flow away before he could finish drinking it.

Hugo had worked with them until his part was discovered in a scandal organized by their former boss, Georges Morvan. He had been dismissed from the diplomatic service, but hired as a banker with Credit Lyonnaise, a French bank with offices in London.

"What did he have to say?" Raoul asked.

"Walpert was killed outside a notorious gambling hall in New Cross," Gabriel said.

Raoul knew that but wanted clarification. "Do you mean the boxing ring?"

"*Bien sur*," Gabriel said. "Everyone who goes there bets on the outcome of the fights. Some win, some lose. Walpert was one of the losers. Hugo says there may be a chance that he stole from the bank to pay his debts."

"And that Rothschild arranged his death?" Raoul scoffed. "Banks do not operate that way. More likely Walpert would have been prosecuted and sent to the poorhouse."

"But what if he stole money that was intended for the Suez Canal?" Gabriel persisted. "That could cause a diplomatic incident. Better to remove Walpert quickly."

Raoul shuddered at his colleague's dark imagination.

Later that day, he reviewed the afternoon's post with Alexandre and Gabriel. The three of them were young and handsome, good dancers, and in possession of the appropriate formal wear to attend soirées and dinner parties. The embassy considered it appropriate to support charitable affairs, especially those with a connection to the French community, and at least once a week one or more of them were drafted to dine and dance.

"Here is an interesting invitation," Alexandre said, holding up a piece of heavy card paper. "A dinner in support of the Soup Kitchen for the Jewish Poor at Spitalfields."

"Why should we be invited to such an event?" Gabriel asked.

"The chief sponsor of the facility is a French Jewess named Rebecca Curiel," Alexandre said. "Wife of the boxer who has been arrested for the murder of Mr. Walpert."

"How do you know that?" Raoul asked.

"One of my schoolmates at the Ecole Supérieure de Commerce de Paris was a Jewish fellow, who has come to work here in London for Credit Foncier. I see him on occasion, and I know he and his mortgage bank are one of the organization's donors."

"Interesting," Raoul said.

"My friend has mentioned to me that in the past Mrs. Curiel has funded a great deal of the soup kitchen's efforts from her own purse, or her husband's winnings in the boxing arena. However the need has grown greater with the influx of all these German and Russian Jews, so she must be looking for additional sources of funds."

"It is a charity, run by a Frenchwoman," Raoul said. "I suggest that we request the office to purchase tickets for us."

"You don't intend us to socialize with Jews!" Gabriel said, scandalized.

"They do not bite, as far as I know," Raoul said. "And Alexandre here went to college with one of them. I see no reason to refuse support to a French-affiliated charity simply because of who it serves."

"My friend is quite a pleasant fellow," Alexandre said. "I can see if he will be attending this dinner, and arrange to be seated with him."

"You may count me out," Gabriel said.

"I for one am interested in this charity, and in meeting your friend, Alexandre," Raoul said. "Please make the arrangements. And now let us continue to review the correspondence."

As they went through further letters and requests, Raoul kept part of his mind on Rebecca Curiel. If her charity was struggling for funds, what might she do to secure them? Agree to make an accusation against her husband?

Chapter 28

Dinner

Silas

Silas found it odd that instead of heading for Bryanston Mews by himself after the close of business on Monday, he accompanied Pemberton in a carriage to Ormond Yard.

Their carriage arrived just as John and Raoul approached on foot. The four of them entered together, and Will announced that Mr. Curiel was already in the lounge with Lord Dawson and Mr. Marsh.

Silas caught Ezra's eye as they entered, and he felt such a pain in his heart as he had never experienced before. Though Ezra did not appear in ill health, there was something of defeat in his face, and Silas longed to rush forward and comfort him. But the way that Ezra looked down, and wrapped his arms around his broad chest, held him back.

"Who would like a whisky?" Magnus asked, and he then busied himself at the bar as everyone sat down.

The room was comfortable, much more so than Silas's single room. The sofa and chairs were upholstered with a subtle pattern of tropical birds, a nod to Magnus's time in warm climates while in the Navy. The curtains were fine silk, the rug on the floor an ornate oriental that showed only the tiniest signs of wear.

It was a room, and a home, that Silas realized he ached for.

"It has been a long day for everyone, I imagine," Toby said. "So we will eat first, and fortify ourselves, and then discuss things."

They all took their whisky glasses and proceeded into the dining room, where Will and Carlo had set the table for seven. The first course was the same soup Carlo had served at Sylvia's birthday, a meat broth with tiny shreds of egg in it, and everyone pronounced delicious. It was followed by thinly sliced veal sautéed with mushrooms and a Madeira sauce, and roasted potatoes and carrots.

"I'll start, because I probably have the least to offer," Silas said, after Will had cleared the last of the plates away. "I received a photo of Mr. Walpert from Antony Wigton's office."

He passed the photograph around. Ezra received it and nodded. "I have spoken with him often before fights," he said. "He was a fellow Jew, and sought to use that connection to influence his betting. He would ask how I was feeling, if I had any particular aches or pains that might influence my fight strategy, and so on. My understanding was that when I began fighting, he bet on me to win regularly, whether the odds were long or short." He looked down at the table. "He called me his lucky talisman."

He opened the top button of his shirt and tugged out a palm-shaped charm on a gold chain from around his neck. "This is a hamsa," he said, showing it around. "Thought to bring good luck by the Jews of North Africa. When he saw mine, he immediately purchased one for himself." He frowned. "Though it clearly did not bring him luck."

"When I spoke with him, he said he was a follower of yours," Silas said. "I didn't realize he had gone quite so far, though."

"We know that Walpert was a gambler," Pemberton said. "It is possible that someone from his bookie's assaulted him, not expecting Walpert to fall to his death."

"Raoul and I may be able to add to that," John said. "We went over to New Cross and spoke to a number of men. I was warned not to travel around the boxing arena at night after there have been fights, because thieves and footpads prey on men who've had too much to drink and might have a few coins in their pocket as the result of a good wager."

"And I spoke with a hustler of about Walpert's age, who says they were at a Ragged School together," Raoul said. "And that if he hadn't been so good at numbers, Walpert could have ended up like him, sucking men for money."

He hesitated, then continued. "Some of you might recall my former colleague, Hugo Malherbe, who is a man like us and has been a guest at one of the soirées. He lost his job at the embassy when Morvan was dismissed, and went to join a French bank. I heard through another colleague who spoke with Hugo that many bankers knew of Walpert's gambling problems, and there was some suspicion that the Rothschilds themselves might be behind his death, if he betrayed them somehow."

Silas copied that information down, as Pemberton complimented Raoul and John on the intelligence.

Raoul continued, "I also heard that Rebecca has been funding her charity in large part herself, and that it is need of funds to continue its work."

"That explains it!" Ezra said. "I have been noticing money missing from our household accounts. I have meant to discuss it with Rebecca, but I was waiting for the right moment. I did not want to challenge her too harshly."

Toby picked up the trail. "I met with Gervase Quinn this morning and he was already aware of the case against Ezra, and the possible diplomatic complications."

"What does that mean?" Ezra asked.

Magnus stepped in. "If we begin with the premise that you did not punch Nathan Walpert and cause his death, then someone else must have. It is left to us, then, to discover who threw that fatal punch, and why."

Toby continued, "Quinn is worried that Walpert might have sold intelligence about the purchase of the Suez canal shares, or been paid by someone to look for ways to scuttle it or cause problems with the numbers."

"The ideas people have." Pemberton shook his head. "Let us recap what we have learned. There are at least several directions I could turn this case. First, I can direct aspersions against Walpert's integrity. That someone might have tried to take advantage of his connection to the Suez deal, and that led to his murder."

Silas wrote that down with a big number one. He was beginning to feel better about Ezra's chances before the puisne judge.

"Second, we have Walpert's propensity to gamble," Pemberton said. "Although it is unusual to kill a man over debts, because the bookmaker loses the opportunity to collect. But it is possible that someone threatened Walpert and his death was an accidental result of that threat."

Magnus said, "Yesterday I spoke with a wine merchant we often purchase from, Samuel Steingrob. Do you know him, Ezra?"

"Only from the shul," he said. "Rebecca handles all the household purchases and accounts."

Silas saw a twinkle in Magnus's eye as he said, "He complained about many of your countrymen. Apparently those of your background think they are better than the Eastern Europeans like himself."

Ezra shrugged. "That is the way of some. If I am distant, it is because I have less interest in religion than others."

"He said that he knew Walpert from your shul, and that he thought he was a gambler. He spoke very disparagingly of men in illegal businesses like prostitution and gambling. He also gave me the name of a man called Bertie Greenbaum."

Ezra shivered, as if a chill had come into the room. "Greenbaum has approached me on occasion, implying that if I were able to control the outcome of a certain bout, there would be a great deal of money in it for me. I always refused."

Silas was relieved. Aside from the lies that had to be told by men of their ilk, he had felt Ezra to be honorable, and he was glad to have that confirmed.

Pemberton turned to Ezra. "Then we come to the question of your wife. Why would she step forward and lie to Scotland Yard about your whereabouts on the night of the murder, and go so far as to mention blood on your clothing?"

"I have thought about this a great deal," Ezra said. "As you can imagine, I had hours of solitary confinement with my thoughts my only companions."

He sighed. "Neither of us married for love. My father understood I was only interested in boxing, to the exclusion of anything else, even women. Though he did not know of my inclinations, he despaired that I would never marry."

His hand shook noticeably, and Silas wanted to reach over and comfort him. He explained the circumstances of their marriage, and the men around him nodded in understanding. "There are many men who would see such accommodation," Magnus said. "And I know several who already live in such a way."

"Can you see a way she could profit from your incarceration?" Pemberton asked.

Ezra shrugged. "She expects a large inheritance from her father, who is in ill health in Paris," he said. "Her father settled some money on us when we married, which enabled us to move to London and purchase the house in Hackney. Because of the laws about women and money, it is in my name. Though it has been pledged against my freedom, if I stand trial, it is released, no?"

"That's correct," Pemberton said. "And if you are imprisoned, she takes control of all your assets. Do you have investments? Company shares, other real estate?"

"I was fortunate in my early career in France to win significant money in prize fights," Ezra said. "My father invested that carefully for me, and kept me on a tight budget. Rebecca was raised by a rich father who allowed her a lavish allowance and was very generous to the poor, and she has continued that effort. Until now, I believed that she was directing her own funds that way, but now I worry that she may be overspending her accounts."

He shook his head. "But we still maintain a substantial bank balance. In London, many men have been eager to secure my acquaintance, and offer me the opportunity to invest in various enterprises."

He quoted them a figure which astonished Silas, and apparently most of the other men, as the current total of his fortune. "Though if I am not careful Rebecca will give it all away. She insists that she must make large donations to charities to enhance her social position."

"I sent a message to the Honorable Sylvia Cooke yesterday, asking her to pay a call on Mrs. Curiel, whom she had met through one of those charities," Magnus said. "She and Miss Cleaver did, and then Toby and I spoke with them."

"Your friends met with my wife?" Ezra said with surprise. "She has said in the past that she had acquaintance with several women of nobility but I dismissed that as fantasy. How was she? She was not at home when I returned from prison. I changed my clothes and came here before she returned."

"Sylvia said that she seemed surprisingly cheerful for a woman whose husband was in gaol. She wore a pink dress rather than to appear in mourning."

"I am not surprised."

"Miss Cleaver also mentioned that she overheard a woman speak of 'that awful Mr. Greenbaum.' Does your wife have connection with him?"

"I didn't think so." He thought for a moment, and then his mouth opened wide. "The money that has gone missing from our household accounts. Is it possible that she has been betting with Greenbaum?"

He stood up abruptly. "I must get to the bottom of this!"

Chapter 29

Life at Stake

Silas

Silas looked up in alarm at Ezra, towering over him.

"Sit, please, Mr. Curiel," Pemberton said. "This is but one part of the puzzle. You must promise to refrain from action until we have everything assembled."

Ezra sat, and Pemberton looked around at the group of men. "Now, is there anything we have not covered?"

"Will and I went through the guest list for you," Magnus said. He withdrew a piece of paper from his jacket and handed it to Silas. "There was a wide selection of guests at various times. Not all inverts."

"Very good," Pemberton said. "That will be useful if we need to call witnesses to Ezra's presence here and establish his alibi."

Eventually they were all dismissed. "I don't wish to return to Hackney," Ezra told Silas as they walked out to Ormond Yard. "I am afraid that if I see Rebecca I will be very angry with her, and that would only encourage her to reiterate her claims against me."

"You will come to my room with me," Silas said, and put his hand on Ezra's arm.

They walked through the darkened streets together. "You don't believe the allegations against me, do you?" Ezra asked.

"If I did, would I marshal my friends and my employer to assist in your defense?" Silas said. "Of course I do not."

"While I was imprisoned, I thought of you," Ezra said. He smiled. "How you would decorate even a dank cell with your scarves and your pictures. How you can make any place you are seem like a home, and any man in your arms feel safe and loved."

"You would never be comfortable in a tiny room such as mine," Silas said. "Where would you exercise?"

"If I am found innocent, we will address the manner of our living," Ezra said. "Surely with my help you can find a better place to live."

"The better the place, the more the eyes upon us," Silas said. "At least in my room, no one knows you are there."

They arrived at Silas's room, and because both were exhausted, they did little more than cuddle before both fell asleep.

Tuesday morning, Ezra left early to return to his regular workout routine. Silas pulled his collar up around his neck as he walked out into the December chill, his nose full of the smell of coal and wood smoke. The fog was thick as pea soup, muffling the sound of carriage wheels on cobblestone streets and the pealing of church bells calling the faithful to early morning services.

On his way to the Inns of Court, he passed houses decorated with wreaths and garlands made of evergreen branches, holly, and mistletoe on their doors and windows, reminding him that Christmas was coming. What would Ezra do during the holidays, he wondered? Surely his household would not celebrate.

Silas felt a pang of nostalgia for his childhood, when his father brought in a small tree and he and his mother and sister decorated it. The thrill of waking on Christmas morning to see what Father Christmas had brought him. Perhaps a wooden toy or the exotic taste and smell of an orange.

He shook those thoughts away. His sister would be grown by now, and he doubted his parents would do much to celebrate.

Even though it was still early, he arrived to find Luke outside. The boy was practicing some form of exercise, though awkwardly. "I shall give you your own key," Silas said. "There is no reason for you to wait outside if you are the first to arrive."

"It's all right," Luke said. "I'm doing my boxing practice."

"Are you an aficionado of that sport, then?" Silas asked, as he unlocked the door.

"Don't know what that means," Luke said.

"A fan," Silas said. "Do you want to box yourself someday?"

"We had a man at school who taught us self-defense for a while," Luke said. "Said it was good to keep our bodies strong, and also in case someone tried to hurt us."

Silas watched as Luke made the tea. The boy was shaping up well.

Pemberton was in court, so Silas spent the morning copying out his notes from the previous evening and trying to make sense of what came next. There was an inflammatory article in the *Times* about the Suez deal, and though there was no mention of Nathan Walpert, it was clear that his death was continuing to stir up trouble.

Silas spent a great deal of time understanding the specifics of the deal—who was to pay what when, how the Rothschild bank came in, and what Disraeli's larger goals might be. While there were many elements he didn't fully understand, he could not make a case that Walpert might have had access to specialized information, or that his death was in any way connected to the deal.

"He was just a banker," he told Pemberton that afternoon. "Little more than a clerk. He had some training in accounts and had a good head for numbers, but I can't find anything that suggests he had special access to information which he might have traded or sold."

"Wasn't there a suggestion from someone Raoul spoke with that Walpert might have had a tendency for men?" Pemberton asked. "Could he have repressed his desires so long that they exploded that night and he offered his mouth to someone, as way to gain coin toward his debts, and that man reacted badly?"

Silas wondered for a moment if that might describe Pemberton himself. As far as he knew, Pemberton was not active in his desires. "That might fit in with what Gerard Houghton saw," he said.

Pemberton went into his office and Silas returned to his desk. Late in the afternoon a message arrived from Toby Marsh, which Silas read and then took into Pemberton's office.

"There was some mention in the *Times* this morning of the Suez deal, but nothing that concerned Walpert's death," Pemberton said after he read it. "This message from Marsh indicates the Foreign Office has concluded its investigation, with the same result."

"What does that mean for our case?"

"It means that one of our avenues of interest has run into a dead end."

Silas felt an emptiness in his stomach as he walked back to his desk. He still believed fervently that Ezra was innocent, but he began to worry that Pemberton would be unable to provide enough evidence to convince a judge.

He looked through the paperwork for the case and found Ezra's home in Hackney. Could he dare go there? Perhaps find a boy to take a message up to the door, asking Ezra to meet him nearby? There was no indication of where Ezra worked out during the day, and it was possible he wouldn't even be home.

Silas dithered for the rest of the afternoon, finally giving in. He had to see Ezra and talk to him, to learn how his lover felt and reassure himself that the bond he felt was not all in his imagination.

He set out to walk to Ezra's home, making a few turns until he reached Old Street, which should take him most of the way. It was farther than he thought, and after nearly an hour had passed and the sun had dropped, he began to worry that he had made a terrible mistake. Suppose he should discover Ezra at dinner with his wife, enjoying a companionship that he had denied?

His footsteps faltered. He should turn around and go home.

But no, he had come this far. He had to continue.

He came to Mare Street, which he knew from his map ran

through much of Hackney, and turned onto it. As he approached Tudor Road, where Ezra resided, he smelled the cedar fragrance of cigar smoke in the area—a scent that struck him with memory of the cigar Ezra had smoked as they walked to Ormond Yard the night of the soirée – the night that Nathan Walpert had been murdered.

He followed his nose until he spotted Ezra's distinctive frame ahead of him. "Mr. Curiel?" he said.

Ezra peered forward. "Silas? What in God's name are you doing here?"

"I had to see you," Silas said. "Why are you on the street?"

"I need a good cigar when I am agitated," Ezra said. "The scent calms me. And Rebecca will not allow me to smoke in the house. She says that it makes her sneeze."

He laughed shortly. "Not that she would ever do anything so unladylike as to sneeze or fart, at least not in my presence."

Silas came closer, and Ezra put a hand on his shoulder—perhaps a gesture of fellow feeling, or one that cautioned Silas not to come any closer. They were on Ezra's home turf.

"But you must have a stronger reason to come all this way," Ezra said. "And on foot! Have there been new developments in my case?"

Silas shrugged. "Barrister Pembroke has exhausted one area that might have proved a distraction. The idea that Walpert was killed because of his affiliation with Rothchild's and the Suez canal deal."

"But he still has your testimony," Ezra said. "That you were with me at the party at the time Walpert was killed."

"Indeed. And if necessary he can push Gerard Houghton to state that he saw the assault on Walpert, and it occurred while you and I were at the party."

"Then what worries you?"

He looked at Silas, and then said, "Come with me."

He led Silas down the street, turned a corner, then into an alley, disturbing a cat as they did. Then he gently pushed Silas against the wall and leaned forward to kiss him.

Silas's body relaxed, releasing tension he had only vaguely understood he held. This physical touch was what he needed to remind him of the connection he had to Ezra, and its strength.

They kissed, and their bodies moved together, Silas with his back against the rough brick. But he hardly felt that through his thick overcoat. Instead he was suffused with the warmth of Ezra's breath, his body.

"I wish I could take you back to my house and have my way with you," Ezra said. "But it would not do to bait Rebecca, and give her concrete evidence of the fact that our marriage has ever been a sham."

"I don't want to leave you," Silas said. "Now, or ever."

"Ever is a long time," Ezra said gently. "And there are many hurdles we must conquer before then." He smiled. "Come, let me hail you a carriage. You must get to bed, and rest, to be able to continue to marshal all your forces in my defense."

Wednesday morning, Pemberton came into the office, accompanied by a cold wind, and Luke offered him a mug of tea from the still-warm pot. Robb took Pemberton's coat, and Silas followed Pemberton into his office. "Have you read this morning's *Times*?" Pemberton asked.

"I have," Silas said. "I was surprised that in the announcement of the completion of the financing, there was no mention of Walpert's death."

"That's because no one in any position of power gives our theory any credence," Pemberton said. "As we learned yesterday afternoon from the Foreign Office. And it squashes most of our ideas that Walpert was killed because of his position at Rothschild's. We have no real evidence, only suspicion, and that will carry no weight now that deal is complete."

"What should I do now?"

"I need you to compile a detailed itinerary of Mr. Curiel's movements on the night of the murder. When he arrived at the boxing ring, and the hour his bout finished. How long passed before you met him outside? Then the time of your arrival at the Tabard Inn, with any supporting evidence that he was there. Have you been back to the restaurant since then?"

Silas shook his head.

"Then you must return this evening and quiz the staff. Do they remember seeing the two of you together on the night in question? Is there any detail that might convince Justice Kenyon that Curiel was there at that time?"

"Have you ever been there?" Silas asked.

"The Tabard Inn? On occasion, yes."

"Then you know the barmaid..."

"Is a man in a dress," Pemberton said. "He would not make a very good witness if that information were to come out, and could possibly expose him to prosecution. So ask him what he knows, but try to get corroboration."

"I'll do that."

"And then continue with the rest of the evening. The time you left the Tabard, and your arrival at Ormond Yard. Will is a sharp lad—he'll probably be able to state the approximate time you both arrived."

"And I have the guest list that he and Magnus prepared."

"Good. See if you can put that in order of arrival and departure."

"I'll take care of that."

"And then when you are finished with documenting Mr. Curiel's alibi, I'm afraid you must return to your research on similar cases of manslaughter. Even though we both know he is innocent, we must be prepared for the fact that despite our best efforts, he is declared guilty and I must argue regarding his penalty."

Silas was discouraged, but he returned to his desk and began writing what Pemberton had asked for. By the end of the afternoon, he had done all he could without the help of either Magnus or Will, and he resolved to stop by Ormond Yard on his way to ask questions at the Tabard Inn.

Chapter 30

The Tabard

Toby

Toby was working on a particularly thorny German translation when Will announced that Mr. Warner was at the door. "Show him in," Toby said. He gathered his papers up, glad to have a diversion.

"How goes the defense?" Toby asked, after Will had taken Silas's coast.

"Not well. You saw the *Times* this morning?"

Toby nodded. "Magnus and I wondered how that would affect your plans."

"It has knocked one leg out from under Ezra's defense," Silas said. He explained how Pemberton's strategy was changing. "I was hoping I could speak with Magnus about the guest list."

"He has gone out to dinner at his club," Toby said. "But I'm sure Will and I can do just as well."

He summoned Will, and by putting their heads together, the three of them were able to establish a rough chronology of who had arrived at the salon and when. "When you are ready, I'm sure Magnus will accompany you or Pemberton to interview the guests who might be most willing to testify," Toby said when they were finished.

"Thank you. I don't know what I would do if I didn't have your support."

"What do you do next?"

"Now I must head to the Tabard Inn to see if anyone there can verify seeing Ezra with me that night."

"That will be tricky," Toby said. "Many of the patrons of the Tabard won't want to be identified as connected with the place. And the proprietors could also be nervous if the character of their establishment were to become public knowledge."

"I have to try."

"Well, I have no plans for dinner. Why don't I accompany you? We'll drink and we'll dine and we'll see what kind of information we can discover."

Toby knew he should be distraught over Ezra's plight, but he couldn't help feeling excited about the opportunity to do some sleuthing. He and Magnus had originally been introduced, and joined forces, to investigate a potential situation with international consequences, and though they had seen some excitement since then, the duties of translation were tedious.

He called for his coat and Silas's, and told Will he would be dining out. Then they walked into the cold, fetid air. There was no hint of a breeze, and the smell of chamber pots, privies and horse dung grasped their lungs and would not let go.

"I cannot walk in this air," Toby said. "Let us catch a carriage."

They finally flagged one down on Duke of York Street and gave the driver the intersection nearest the Tabard Inn, in case he should recognize it and refuse to take them there.

"It will all work out," Toby said when they were encased in the relative warmth of the carriage. "Pemberton is one of the best barristers in London. I have heard him argue at a soirée a few times, and he is most convincing."

"I hope so. It seems awful to consider Ezra might be sent to prison for a crime I know he could not have committed."

"You hold him in your heart, don't you?" Toby asked.

Silas sighed. "At first, I thought of him merely as an enjoyable bedfellow. I reveled in his strength, you know. And it was so surprising that a very masculine man such as he would be interested in someone more fey, like myself."

"Our brains cannot overrule our hearts," Toby said. "When I was first introduced to Magnus, we regarded each other with disdain. I thought him a foolish fop, and he viewed me through the lens of class, as a mere servant."

"Yet you overcame those difficulties?"

"We did." Toby smiled. "Going to bed together certainly helped. And when we argue, which we do, Magnus has only to kiss me, or palm my cock, and my disposition changes."

"I have not argued much with Ezra," Silas said. "We have not been together long enough to have exposed our differences. But from the start he has felt different from other men. I am enthralled by his body, of course, but when we talk, it is as if we have known each other for years. And every new detail I learn about him deepens my affection."

The carriage arrived, and they disembarked and Toby paid the fare, over Silas's mild objection. "I could ask Pemberton," Silas said.

"And who do you think pays Pemberton's bills?"

Silas came to a sudden realization, based on the accounts he had begun to manage. "The client."

"Indeed. In this case, that would be Mr. Curiel. I am pleased that the cost of carriage fare is well within my budget, and even though your amour has money now, he may have need of it later."

Toby led the way to the Tabard Inn. He was grateful for his situation, and the ability to make small generous gestures. The truth was that he lived largely on the income from Magnus's investments, though his own work in translating and tutoring gave him pocket money. Without Magnus, he might still be back in Cambridge, struggling to teach unresponsive students about the subjunctive clauses of French.

Jolly Olly appeared surprised to see them. He wiped his hands on his stained white apron, cocked his head for a moment, then asked, "A table for how many?"

"Two, please," Toby said. "And yes, we are not with our regular partners. Just a lads' night out."

Jolly Olly smiled and led them to a table along one wall, where they ordered ale and eel pie. When Olly had a moment of quiet, Toby motioned him over.

"Do you know the boxer Ezra Curiel?" he asked the man.

"I have been here a few times with him," Silas added.

Thus reassured he was not violating a man's privacy, Olly agreed. "Yes, he is quite the figure of a man."

"Do you recall the last time he and I were here together?" Silas asked.

The man thought for a moment. "It was the night Francis knocked a line of piecrusts into the fire," he said. "Do you recall all the smoke?"

Silas was delighted at the memory. "I do indeed," he said, with a smile.

"Are you aware that Mr. Curiel has been charged with murder?" Toby asked.

"A terrible thing," Olly said.

Silas nodded. "And the thing is, the murder happened at the very time he and I were dining here."

"Really?"

"Indeed." He paused, marshalling his words. "I am the clerk for Barrister Richard Pemberton, who has undertaken Ezra's defense. It may be necessary in court to establish that he and I were here at that time. Would you be willing to appear before the court and make a statement to that effect?"

"I don't know," Olly said.

"Oy, fat man!" the barmaid called. "Orders up!"

"I have to go," Olly said, and he hurried away.

"Can he be made to appear?" Toby asked Silas.

"I believe so. But it may take Pemberton's skill to convince him, and guarantee that no undue attention will be paid to him or his establishment."

Toby smiled. "Or to the barmaid, who at this very moment has slapped Jolly Olly's buttocks."

"In a gesture I am sure is one of affection," Silas said. "Some men are known to enjoy such paddling."

Toby laughed. "I attended a public school, so I am aware of that tradition," he said. "Though for myself I find the resulting redness and discomfort outweighs any momentary pleasure."

"There are creams for that," Silas said. "And the application of those can be as enjoyable as the flat of a hand smacked against tender skin."

"I'll leave that to you and Ezra," Toby said.

"Oh, no, Ezra is much too concerned about the effect of his strength to apply a hand to anyone in the name of pleasure. I speak solely of past experience."

They talked and laughed through another round of ale, and as they ate their pies. By the time they left, Silas was sure that Jolly Olly could be persuaded to testify, even if his palm had to be greased by Pemberton—or eventually Ezra.

Chapter 31

Rebecca

Silas

Thursday morning, Silas met with Pemberton to discuss the progress of the case. "Do you think you will be able to convince Mr. Houghton to testify?" he asked. "He is a solid member of society whom the judge is likely to believe, don't you think?"

"He will be a difficult nut to crack, because of his past experience with the police," Pemberton said. "The queen's counsel may choose to impugn his reputation. And he has no gainful employment, merely living off a family inheritance. He could easily be presented as a louche character not to be believed."

"What about Jolly Olly?" Silas asked. "He is a business owner, and he has a clear recollection of the evening when Walpert was murdered."

"It will be difficult to convince him to testify," Pemberton admitted. "But I am more concerned that questions will arise about the character of the Tabard and its ownership and clientele. It is possible that the judge will be skeptical of such a witness."

Silas must have looked crestfallen, because Pemberton clapped him on the shoulder. "Do not lose heart yet, my boy. We will keep gnawing away at this situation."

Silas's mood improved considerably when Ezra arrived at Pemberton's office in high spirits, accompanied by Antony Wigton. He was excited but at the same time sad. "A police detective came to our house a short time ago," he said. "He wanted to quiz Rebecca further on her statement that I had come home after the fight, with blood on my clothes."

Both men hung their coats on pegs, and accepted mugs of tea. "As soon as he was finished, I spoke with Rebecca, and then went to Mr. Wigton's office to notify him."

"Mrs. Curiel's testimony has come into question, and without it, the whole case against Mr. Curiel begins to crumble," Wigton said. "But I shall let Mr. Curiel tell you."

Both men accepted mugs of tea and Silas noted the way Ezra wrapped his cold hands around the warm pottery. Then he took a long draw.

Silas was eager to hear everything, but it was up to Pemberton to ask the questions.

"What did Mrs. Curiel tell the detective?" Pemberton asked.

"The detective took her into another room, so I did not hear their conversation. But after he left Rebecca confessed to me. The detective pressured her as to why she would give false evidence against her own husband." He took a deep breath. "She told him it was because she has borrowed money from a scoundrel called Bertie Greenbaum in order to finance her charitable work. She is quite deeply in debt. He agreed to release her debt if she cooperated with him."

"You mentioned the other night that money was disappearing from your household accounts," Silas said. "So that is believable."

Ezra sipped his tea again. "She also said that she was willing to betray me because I was an invert."

Silas scanned Wigton's face to see if this was news to the solicitor, but could not read him. Perhaps any surprise had passed back at his own office.

"Did this detective say or do anything else before he left?" Pemberton asked.

Ezra shook his head. "Do you think the police will press charges against me for sodomy or some other sexual crime?"

Wigton said, "What happens regularly is that when a man of some wealth or class is arrested for sodomy, he is kept incarcerated for a few days, then let free with a sneer. The number of men who are charged with a crime is small, and few are brought to trial."

He smiled at Ezra. "Without direct evidence, there is little reason for the police to bring charges against you. Have you ever brought a man to your home in Hackney?"

"Never."

"And to your knowledge, has your wife or anyone else ever seen you in flagrante with another man?"

"I have been very careful." He sighed. "Though obviously not careful enough."

Pemberton nodded. "I will request a hearing in front of Justice Kenyon to see about having the charge of murder dropped against you. At that point the police may decide to shift the charge to one of indecent behavior, but my belief is that they will cut you loose."

"I will be free?" Ezra asked in surprise.

"Free of the murder charge," Pemberton said. "But you must understand that once the police learn a piece of information, it passes around the force and into the general public. Especially when it is something as salacious as this."

"You can hold your head up high," Silas said. "You have always been proud. Simply continue that."

"It will not be that easy," Wigton said. "I doubt you shall be able to box again professionally, at least not in London, perhaps not in all of England."

"My abilities have not changed!" Ezra said.

"But the crowd will be against you," Silas said. "You saw it with Fullham, did you not? After he fainted during his bout with you, the crowd began calling him a woman. Even though he sustained himself in two other subsequent fights, his name has been removed from the lists."

"But boxing is all I have!" Ezra said.

"It is possible that crowds on the continent will be more forgiving," Pemberton said. "You are French, after all, so perhaps your countrymen will rally around you."

Silas could only imagine how this news would affect Ezra. For himself, he felt as if the contents of his stomach wanted to rise up. To see Ezra's name cleared, and then blackened again in the space of minutes was pain enough. To realize that the thing to which Ezra had devoted his life was to be snatched away from him was even more horrifying.

Even Pemberton's attempts hurt Silas. He knew how important boxing was to Ezra, how he had forsworn nearly everything else in his life in his pursuit of physical excellence. He would not give that up so easily. He already had plans to go to France, and if he was able to box there he might never return.

"What of Mrs. Curiel?" Silas asked. "Will she be prosecuted for giving false evidence?"

"I don't believe we should advocate for that," Pemberton said. "We don't want to draw this case out any longer than we must, nor create additional gossip. Antony, can you speak with the police about that?"

Wigton agreed to do so, and after draining the last of his tea, he regained his coat and left.

"Silas, you must draft a request for a hearing to review the charges against Mr. Curiel," Pemberton said. "You will find examples in Cyril's files. I will review and sign it, and we'll have Robb deliver it."

"I can work on that," Silas said.

"If the judge does not consent to release Ezra, at least this morning's information has given us another direction to pursue. Did you discern anything we did not discuss with Wigton?"

Ezra stood silently as Silas thought back over their conversation.

Suddenly, it came to him. "Why would Bertie Greenbaum use his leverage over Rebecca to implicate Ezra?"

"Indeed." He turned to Ezra. "Have you had any dealings at all with Greenbaum?"

"None whatsoever. I have spoken to him on occasion and rejected his offers. Do you think that is why he has it in for me? If he removes me from the ring, he may be able to persuade whoever takes my place."

"That is an interesting idea," Pemberton said. "Silas, make a note of that, and let's see if we can dig up anything useful about the other boxers at New Cross?"

"There's another possibility," Silas said. "Could it be that Greenbaum or one of his minions had something to do with Walpert's death? That by shifting the blame to Ezra he protects himself?"

"Another intriguing idea," Pemberton said. "You have a very good head on your shoulders, my boy. You are going to make an excellent head clerk."

Silas basked in the praise, while his mind spun forward with ideas about Greenbaum's motives.

"Why might Greenbaum take an interest against you?" he asked Ezra. "Could there be a religious motive? How do your people feel about engaging in contact sports such as boxing?"

"When I first contemplated a career as a boxer, my father asked advice of the most scholarly rabbi in Paris," Ezra said. "He said that Jewish law categorizes risk taking into three categories: minimal, moderate, and high risk. In boxing, there is a high risk of injury to oneself, as well as injury to another. He advised that I should step away from the ring unless I had no other way of earning a living. Since I did not want to become a manual laborer, I felt I had no other choice."

He smiled. "Besides, I loved the sport. Still do. And as far as the religion I share with Greenbaum, he ought to be more concerned about his own soul. From what I understand, the occasional bet is allowed if in a frivolous pursuit, such as children do when playing with the dreidel, a top spun at Hanukkah where the wagers are pennies or candies. But if gambling is connected to thievery, as Greenbaum does, then it's prohibited at all times. Which is why I will never accept money to affect the outcome of a match."

"Duly noted," Pemberton said. Then he turned to Silas. "We should send notes to our allies as well, telling them of our progress. Before you begin the dismissal request, can you write those notes up and have Robb deliver them?"

Silas agreed, and Ezra accompanied him to his desk. "I don't know where I shall go," Ezra said. "I can't return to Hackney to live with Rebecca, knowing what she has done to me."

"Then you must pack up your clothes and toiletries and come to my room," Silas said. "It is small but it can accommodate us in the short term." He took a deep breath. "Until you leave for Paris."

"My father will not welcome me after this news," Ezra said. "This will all be my fault—the murder charge, the damage to Rebecca's reputation." He held up his hand. "I know, I know, she was the one who borrowed beyond her means and lied. But it will be down to me. If I had been a better husband she would never have done those things."

"I must write my notes," Silas said. "You go to Hackney, and then to Bryanston Mews, and we will see what's what."

Then, in full view of Luke and Robb, he leaned forward and kissed Ezra on the lips. "I will be beside you, *mon amour*."

Luke did not say anything, but Silas was sure they would speak of it when he was not there. Perhaps it would upset Luke enough that he would leave his position. So be it.

Chapter 32

Choices

Raoul

R aoul was surprised when Beller announced that Mr. Warner was at the door. "Is there news?" he asked, as he jumped up to greet his friend.

"Good and bad," Silas said, as he handed his coat to Beller. Once the valet was out of the room, they embraced, and Silas could not help himself. He began to sob.

"Oh, no, tell me," Raoul said. "Ezra is not to hang, is he?"

"No," Silas choked out. He struggled to control his tears as he sat on the plump divan and told Raoul all that had transpired that day. "I need to go home, but I must think about what to say to Ezra before I do."

"This calls for alcohol," Raoul said. "I have an excellent apple brandy from Calvados. May I pour you a glass?"

"Yes, please," Silas said. He blew his nose with his handkerchief and leaned forward on the divan when Raoul handed him an elegant snifter with deep brown brandy in it. He lifted it to his nose, inhaled the fragrance, and then sipped. The liquid forged a warm path down his throat and began the process of settling him.

"Suppose he were to go to France," Raoul asked. "Would you go with him?"

"What would I do? I don't even know the language."

Raoul shrugged. "Be his kept man."

"I don't think Ezra would want that. Nor would I. I am too accustomed to looking after myself."

"Sometimes you must make compromises," Raoul said. "I went from my father's house to Father Maurice's bed, and then at the priest's direction went to university. I thought I had begun to gain my independence there, but now that I look back I was under the direction of my professors. And then when I came to London, I was Morvan's man."

"But you changed. You stood up to him."

Raoul smiled. "I did. And then I moved in with John." He waved his hand around the elegantly appointed room.

Silas recognized that it was fancier than Magnus and Toby's, with fine china on display in a cabinet, rich Oriental rugs on the floor, not a mote of dust anywhere. Far nicer than anywhere he had lived, or had the expectation of living. "And do you see that as giving up your independence?" he asked.

"In a way. This is John's home, and he covers all the household expenses. Beller is his servant, not mine. I endeavor to pay when we dine out, but sometimes John insists that he simply has more money than I do, so it is more sensible for him to pay."

"And does it suit you, this domesticity? Do you ever long to feel another man's cock in your mouth or your arse?"

"I have complicated feelings about sex, as you know," Raoul said. "The years as Father Maurice's catamite scarred me in many ways. It is hard for me to find joy in sex—except with John, who understands me. And John had enough of bad usage when he was at school. So no, neither of us long for other men. Do you?"

Silas squirmed uncomfortably on the divan. "I used to feel my cockstand rise every time a man looked at me. But since I met Ezra I can never find a man to compare."

"And how does he feel about you?"

"We do not talk much, just fuck and cuddle," Silas said. "Though he did say that he appreciates that I have stood by him and recruited you all to help him." He took another sip of the warm brandy. With his eyes closed, he could almost imagine those were Ezra's lips touching his, and he smiled, to think of his lover and someone he could savor and consume.

"I think you are jumping ahead," Raoul said. "As you said, you have only been together a few months. If he chooses to go to France, that will be his choice. If he does not ask you to accompany him, that will be a clear statement of his feelings."

Silas's heart flip-flopped once more. "And what if he does?"

"Then you will have to make a decision. You are new in your career with Pemberton. Do you still want to be his clerk thirty years from now? Do you want to risk losing that career to follow a man's arse, no matter how comely it is?"

"I was loose with my affections for so many years, and have only been faithful to Ezra for months."

"Does he expect that?" Raoul asked.

"We have never talked about it. But you and John do not stray, and I don't believe that Magnus and Toby do either."

"We are but two couples," Raoul said. "And we have made our own way. Men of our ilk do not have society dictating what we choose. As long as we are circumspect we are able to make the choices that suit us. You and Ezra must do the same."

"I worry about all the pressure on him," Silas said. "From his father, his wife, the boxing organizers and fans, even his co-religionists."

"And you fear that you will come last in that list?" Raoul asked gently.

"I guess I do."

"Then you must wait and see what choices Ezra makes."

Chapter 33

Independence

Silas

Silas made his solitary way home. He did not know if Ezra would take him up on his offer to share his room. It was small, after all, without any of the modern conveniences of the house in Hackney. He had to share a backyard privy with a dozen other tenants, while Ezra and Rebecca had running water and a new kind of indoor toilet. From what he understood, on the ground floor Rebecca had a salon, a dining room and a kitchen, much like Magnus and Toby had, and there were three bedrooms upstairs: one for Rebecca, one for Ezra, and a third for guests.

Rebecca cooked for herself and Ezra, and a maid came in every day to clean. It was altogether a much higher lifestyle than that which Silas could afford.

What if Ezra could no longer box? What would he do for the next twenty or thirty years of his life? Even if he went to France to box, his body would only hold out for so long. Ezra had admitted he was not much of a scholar, though he did seem to have some head for business, investing his proceeds in funds. How long would that last him?

His room was empty when he returned to it. He sat on his bed, and the colored scarves above it, which had once seemed so joyous, now were pitiful and somewhat tattered. He was lost in his own misery when he heard a loud rapping at the door.

He rose to answer it, and Ezra swooped in, and grabbed him in an embrace. Ezra's kiss was so happy that Silas had no choice but to respond in kind. When they finally came apart, he was almost dizzy.

"What has caused this change in your manner?" he asked.

"When I arrived at the house in Hackney I discovered a note Rebecca left me. She cannot bear the humiliation I have caused her. She has taken herself off to her father's house in Paris. She will make no claim against the house or my assets if I do not reveal the circumstances of our breakup to her family, or mine."

"Will you be able to keep that a secret?"

"If I remain in London and keep my profile low," he said. "It is possible that people here will relay the information to others in Paris, but it will only be hearsay if neither of us address it. The other condition is that I appear before a panel of rabbis and grant her a religious divorce."

"And will you do that?"

"Of course!" He picked Silas up by the waist and swung him around. "It means I am free to live my life."

He pressed his groin against Silas's. Silas felt his stiffness and responded in kind, and Ezra let him down. They kissed and rubbed against each other until Silas said, "I don't want to waste your spend inside your trousers." He backed away and began to undo Ezra's belt. Ezra leaned down and kissed the top of his head, and Silas felt ready to burst with joy.

As soon as he had Ezra's trousers open, he reached into his drawers and grabbed his cock, bringing it out. Ezra groaned in pleasure as Silas dropped to his knees and took the long shaft in his mouth, feeling again the unfamiliar sensation of a lack of foreskin.

He took that opportunity to swipe his tongue up and down Ezra's shaft, then swallowed the tip and began stroking the length of it. It didn't take Ezra long to spend, and Silas did his best to swallow all of it.

Then he backed off, and caught his breath.

"I did not come here for sex," Ezra said, when he had finished. "Though of course that is pleasant."

Silas sat on the bed. "Why, then?"

"To take you to your new home, in Hackney," Ezra said. "That is, if you will join me there. You can still walk to the Inns of Court, or take a carriage if the weather is foul. And we have the house to ourselves, so we need not worry about prying eyes or the ears of nosy neighbors."

Silas was astonished. "What about your fights in France?" he asked.

"Those will have to be postponed, until I know better what my reception will be. At some point I must return to Paris to face the Bet Din, the panel of rabbis, and grant Rebecca her divorce, but it does not have to happen immediately, since neither of us will want to remarry."

"What if the rabbis say no?"

"They don't. They simply authorize a scribe to write a document dissolving the marriage. I sign it and hand it to Rebecca, and it's done."

"And in the meantime? Will you box?"

Ezra shook his head. "I have already been told that I am not welcome at New Cross," he said. "That was based on the murder charge, of course, but I will not press things. Give them some time to forget."

"And eventually the bettors will want the chance once again to put their money on the Hammering Hebrew," Silas said.

"It is to be hoped." Ezra looked around. "Now, what do you need to take with you in the carriage this evening? We can come back another day with a cart if necessary."

"The furniture belongs to the house," Silas said. "Only my clothing and personal belongings."

"We will start with these," Ezra said, touching one of the scarves that hung over the bed. "They will be hung again in Hackney."

Silas smiled. Ezra did seem to understand him.

Silas had a single suitcase which he filled with clothing, and then the rest of his belongings went into several bags. When they were finished, and the scarves had been taken down from over the bed and packed, he looked around.

The room was spare and dismal. He had never been inside Ezra's home, but it had to be better. And he would have Ezra by his side.

They dragged case and bags down to the street, and while Ezra hailed a carriage, Silas took a moment to catch his breath. Everything was moving so quickly and he had the sense that he was riding a horse that had gone out of his control.

He had experienced several upheavals in his life so far. Being discovered by his father and thrust out of the house. Starting over again in his first barrister's office, as little more than an errand boy. Then gaining his first clerkship with another, and finally feeling like he had his footing again.

There had been another fresh start in London, and then yet another when he joined Pemberton's office. Since then things had moved even faster, meeting Ezra and falling in love with him, taking on Cyril's position, then organizing Ezra's defense.

Ezra turned a corner ahead of him, still seeking a carriage. What a fine figure of a man he was. None of the athletes or sportsmen on Silas's walls could compare to him. And for some reason, he loved Silas as Silas loved him. What a wonder the world was!

But there were still more obstacles to overcome, more choices to make. Ezra must be cleared of his charges, and find a way to move forward with his life. In the time since Cyril's death, Silas had come to understand how much more he had to learn to fully occupy the position of Pemberton's chief clerk.

Ahead of him a carriage rounded the corner, and Ezra leaned out the window and waved, and Silas's heart leapt like a fish on the line.

Chapter 34

Until Now

Silas

The carriage pulled up and the driver loaded Silas's case and his bags and boxes onto the back. Silas joined Ezra inside the carriage, sitting close on the tufted seat. "I am very glad you are joining me," Ezra said. "The house has always been a lonely place to me, as Rebecca and I crept around, careful to stay away from each other. I believe things will change with you installed there."

Silas relished the feel of Ezra's thigh close to his own, and leaned back. All the cares of the past weeks seemed to fly past the carriage windows, even though he knew this was merely a brief enchanted moment before the storm clouds continued to gather.

Ezra's house was two stories of golden stone, with a bow window on the ground level and two windows above with white shutters. A small gate opened onto a tiny courtyard, with steps down to a basement level and a half-dozen steps up to the front door. Though Silas knew something of what to expect, he was still awed. It was nicer than anywhere he had ever lived, even back in Sheffield with his family.

It was not fancy by the standards of men like Pemberton, but it was a whole house like that occupied by Magnus and Toby. It was not an elegant neighborhood but not an impoverished one either. The carriage driver carried everything into the courtyard, and then Ezra paid him and he drove off.

"What do you think?" Ezra asked.

"It's marvelous," Silas said.

Ezra laughed. "Not quite. But it is pleasant. Let us get everything inside."

He hefted the heaviest box on his shoulder and walked up to the front door. He touched his fingers to a rectangular plaque beside the door and then kissed them, and then unlocked the door and walked inside.

Silas followed, carrying his suitcase and a pair of bags, though he stopped for a moment to look at the plaque Ezra had kissed with his fingers. It was made of brass, with writing in a foreign alphabet and a glass cylinder attached. It appeared to have a tiny scroll inside the cylinder.

"That is our mezuzah," Ezra said, returned to where Silas had stopped. "It is a commandment from God that we bless our home by placing prayers written on that scroll at our doorpost. We kiss it with our fingers on our coming and going, to bless our lives and our home."

"May I?" Silas asked.

"Of course. This is to be your home, too."

Silas mimicked Ezra's action, touching the plaque with his fingers and then kissing them. He smiled and followed Ezra inside.

The interior of the house was simple—a bare wooden floor, a sitting room to the right and a stair to the upper level in front of him. He set his bags down and Ezra went back outside to fetch the rest.

They left everything in the sitting room and Ezra gave him a quick tour – a dining room that led to a kitchen, and an indoor toilet compartment beside it. "The height of luxury!" Ezra said. "No trekking outside in the middle of the night to relieve yourself!"

They carried Silas's clothes upstairs, to where there were three bedrooms. Ezra opened the first door and said, "This is my room."

It was larger than Silas's room at Bryanston Mews. Ornate plaster swags hung over tall windows that looked out to a garden, and had long drapes gathered at the center. A worn Oriental rug covered most of the wooden floor. But the centerpiece to the room was a large four-poster bed, covered with a spread in a floral pattern. Two large pillows were at the head.

Silas stared at the room. Did Ezra expect him to share such a luxurious space?

"You can stow your things in the chest of drawers. Most of what I own needs to be hung up."

Silas began unpacking his case and placing his clothing in the drawers as Ezra watched. He barely took up two of the drawers before he was finished.

"This is all you have?" Ezra asked.

Silas shrugged. "It is all I ever needed."

"I must have my clothing custom tailored to fit my body," Ezra said. He opened the armoire to show off the rows of shirts, trousers, and jackets, all neatly hung. "And my tailor is always interested in new business, so he encourages me."

Silas shook his head to see the row of suits in different fabrics. "And I considered myself a peacock with a few brightly colored shirts and scarves."

Ezra smiled. "I shall have to see to it that you get some new feathers, my peacock. And now let me show you the rest of the house."

He opened a door across the hall from his room. It held a narrow single bed, an armoire with the doors hung open, and a table with a ewer and bowl. It showed signs of a hurried departure in the irregular patches of dust on the floor.

"Rebecca slept in here," Ezra said, standing in the open doorway. "It was easy to justify to others because the way we were both raised, a man could not touch his wife while she was in her time. And since I did not want to have sex with her, I was happy to let her be on her own."

Silas marveled at the ability to own a home with separate

bedrooms for husband and wife. When he was a boy, his family lived in one room for a while. His parents had the bed, and he and his sister slept on pallets on the floor.

There was one more small room on that floor, which they had set aside for visiting family. "I am thinking with Rebecca gone no one will come to visit," Ezra said. "I might make this up into an exercise room for myself, so that I don't have to go out to the gym when it is cold or wet."

He sighed. "Or if I am no longer welcome where I have gone." Then he smiled at Silas. "Let us check the kitchen and see if Rebecca left anything behind we could eat for supper."

There was bread and cheese and a container of marinated mushrooms, and Ezra opened a bottle of wine. He poured out two glasses. "At least tonight I do not have to worry about getting you home if you drink too much." He raised his glass to Silas, and they clinked them together. "L'chaim," Ezra said. "That is a toast among out people. To life. To our life, together."

Silas felt like his heart might burst with happiness. They ate, and talked, both of them avoiding any conversation about the charges still looming against Ezra, or what the future might hold. Instead they spoke about places in France Ezra loved, where he hoped to take Silas one day. Silas talked about Sheffield.

"Do you think you will ever speak with your family again?" Ezra asked.

Silas shrugged. "I doubt it, while my father still lives. I have been in contact with an aunt, to let her know that I am safe in London, and I recently posted her a letter about my promotion to head clerk. She has been kind in response, though never mentioning anything about my parents or my sister."

Silas yawned, and Ezra followed a moment later. "It has been a long day," Ezra said. He led them back to the large room. "I will wash up for bed."

He began stripping off his clothes, and tossing them onto a counter where Silas presumed the maid picked them up to be washed. He watched in awe as each garment that was removed revealed a new and magnificent set of muscles.

"Are you only watching?" Ezra said. "Don't you need to get ready for sleep?"

"For now I am enjoying the view," Silas said. But in truth he was still terrified of the speed with which his life had changed. Without a thought, he had committed himself to this one man, one cock, one arse. For the rest of his life?

His heart beat more rapidly. No, he could not think of it that way. He cared about Ezra and was excited by their sexual congress, and Ezra needed his support in this difficult time. If things changed between them, he could always leave.

He laughed to himself. And return to squalid rooms, after being spoiled in this manner? He would have to become a barrister himself to be able to afford anything comparable.

No, he would be Ezra's kept man, at least for a while. Raoul had accustomed himself to living at John's teat without problems.

Silas's attention returned to Ezra, as his lover pulled off his undershirt and the marvel of his chest was on display. But he didn't stop there. He kicked off his shoes and removed his socks, and then quickly dropped his trousers and his undershorts.

Silas was open-mouthed as Ezra took the washcloth and soap and began to clean himself. "There is a tub downstairs, but it requires the maid to fill it. So I do this every night before bed," Ezra said. "My father taught me this long ago, when we could not afford to wash our sheets very often, and the habit has stayed with me."

When he finished, his skin glistening with water droplets, he held the washcloth out to Silas. "And you?"

Silas only washed his whole body once a week, if that much, but he followed Ezra's lead. The soap had a faint lavender scent, and while at first he was self-conscious about exposing his body to Ezra, when it was lacking in so many ways, but he found he enjoyed the ritual and focused on it.

Ezra climbed into bed, and motioned Silas to join him. Then he extinguished the candle and the room was filled with a milky darkness, only a tiny bit of light from the night sky. They turned to each other and kissed, and then Ezra settled quickly into sleep.

Silas sat up for a few minutes, wondering at the way his life had changed in a single day. Ezra had swept in and assumed that Silas would want to leave his dismal room and join him in such luxury. If he'd had the chance to think about it, would he have agreed so quickly, and without discussion?

He didn't even know if Ezra had household staff. Would a maid come in and disturb their sleep early in the morning? He wasn't sure what Ezra did all week, between his bouts. Exercise? Sparring?

The thoughts crowded his mind until he, too, was overcome by sleep.

The next morning, Silas woke in confusion. Where was he? It took him a moment to realize that he was in Ezra's bed, in Ezra's house. In all his time in London, he had never slept in a bed other than his own. He had had many lovers, and brought many of them back to his room, but he had never gone to another man's house or slept in his bed.

Until now.

He turned on his side to see Ezra still asleep beside him. One muscular arm had snaked out over the bedspread, and Silas stared fondly at the face of his lover. Once again, he thought that Ezra was not classically handsome—his nose was too large, his jaw too narrow. And yet the sight of that face filled him with warmth. Was this to be his life, waking each morning beside this man?

It pleased him to think so. But he knew they had many obstacles to overcome. He needed to be sure that he could be satisfied with one man's body beside him and not lust for every handsome figure he saw. That he could be sure Ezra would not reject him the way his own father had.

And there was the question of his independence, as he had discussed with Raoul. Could he give up his work with Pemberton, just as he had been promoted, to travel the continent as Raoul's kept man? Could they negotiate any agreement between them that they could sleep with other men when they were apart, yet come back together again?

The complications were endless. He had to empty his bladder, and when he reached for the chamber pot he realized that there was a toilet compartment downstairs, as Ezra had shown him the night before.

He crept quietly down the stairs, worrying that he might disturb some household staff and have to defend his position. But all was quiet.

He marveled at the warmth of the house, so much more comfortable than the unreliable heater at Bryanston Mews. That he didn't have to trek out into the wintry cold to use the privy. Surely this was a life he could get used to quickly.

When he returned from the toilet, Ezra was awake. "What time is it?" he asked.

"A little after seven," Silas said.

"Come back to bed, then. We are still celebrating."

"We will have the whole weekend for that," Silas said. "I must dress and find my way from here to the Inns of Court. And then work."

Ezra pulled the covers back and grabbed his stiff cock, and waggled it. "Can you not work here first?"

"Will you be a demanding taskmaster?" Silas asked with a smile. But he moved over to the side of the bed, and got onto his knees so that Ezra could push his cock into Silas's mouth.

"This is the first time I have had sex in this bed," Ezra said. "I like it. And you make the wait worthwhile."

Silas's heart soared as he sucked and stroked Ezra's cock. Ezra ruffled his hair and the feel of his hand, and his cock, was enough to cause Silas to spend right after Ezra did.

Ezra smiled. "I am glad that fate brought you to me, Silas Warner. And now I will go back to sleep, and see if I dream of you."

Silas washed himself, dressed, and walked in the direction of the

Thames, using his internal compass to find his way to the Inns of Court. It took a longer to walk there than it had from Bryanston Mews, but it didn't matter. It gave him more time to think about what the future might hold.

Chapter 35

A Place to Call Home

Silas

At the close of work on Friday evening, Silas had gone three blocks until he realized that he was heading in the wrong direction, and he had to turn and shift his internal compass toward Hackney. He had brought some papers to show Ezra, and was able to verify the address—which he'd only visited late at night and in Ezra's company.

He arrived and realized that he had no key to the front door. He verified the address once more, then knocked.

A minute passed with no response, and he was baffled. He was sure he was at the right place. And all his belongings were inside, so there was no chance he could simply return to Bryanston Mews.

Finally, Ezra opened the door, wearing an undershirt and a pair of boxing shorts. It was either that, or the delicious aroma floating through the house, that made Silas salivate.

"Come in, sorry, I need to get you a key," Ezra said.

Silas took off his coat and hung it on a peg by the door, then followed Ezra's shapely buttocks down the narrow hallway to the kitchen.

"Are you... cooking?" Silas asked.

"Yes," Ezra said. "I went to the market this morning and shopped while the maid was here. When I was a boy, I often sat in the kitchen while my grandmother cooked, so I learned how to make a roast chicken easily. And I was surprised to find artichokes at the market as well, because I do not usually see them for several months. These must have come by ship from somewhere warm."

"Artichokes? What in the world are they?"

"Ah, they are a delicacy! I cannot wait to show you how to eat one. Right now they are boiling on the stove. Now go and wash your hands, and we will eat soon."

Silas was surprised that the hypermasculine Ezra would deign to enter a kitchen. As a boy, if he'd dared enter his mother's domain he would have been shooed away.

When he arrived at the dining room table, Ezra had set it with what looked like good china and silver, and two crystal glasses. A bottle of red wine sat beside a golden braided loaf of bread. "We would usually light a pair of special candles as well, but that is the job of the woman, and Rebecca took with her the silver candlesticks we were given at our wedding."

He motioned Silas to sit, and stood at the head of the table. "This is a custom of my people on Friday night," he said. "Before we eat our meal, we thank God for our bread and wine." He recited a prayer in a language Silas assumed was Hebrew and then he toasted Silas with his wine glass. Then he said a second prayer and broke two pieces of bread, one for each of them.

"Did you bake this, too?" Silas asked. It was delicious, light and airy with a taste of eggs.

Ezra shook his head. "No, I went to a Jewish baker for that. It is a skill beyond me."

After the bread and wine, Ezra presented him with a large green globe, with spiky leaves tinted purple at the edges. "How do you eat this?" Silas asked.

"You peel a leaf like so," Ezra demonstrated. "You dip it in the vinaigrette, which is a simple mixture of olive oil, vinegar, and mustard. Then you run your teeth over it to release the fibers inside."

The way that Ezra opened his mouth and bared his teeth over the leaf was so sensual that Silas found his cock stiffening. He followed Ezra's demonstration and enjoyed the savory taste. "See! I am educating your English palate," Ezra said.

Silas laughed and peeled another leaf. They ate together and Silas was surprised at how sensual it could be to eat a meal with your lover, away from any prying eyes.

Then Ezra served the chicken, which was tender and moist with some kind of exotic flavor Silas had never tasted before. "I could become spoiled by this," Silas said. "Do you often eat this way?"

Ezra shook his head. "Rebecca cooked, and often on a Friday night we were invited to the homes of people from the shul. Or if I was boxing on an early card, I ate something at a pub near the arena." He frowned. "But I won't be going there again for a while."

"You must exercise, though," Silas said. "To keep up your strength."

"I know. But I will have to find somewhere to do that where they don't know me. Or where they don't care who I am."

They finished dinner, and Silas scrubbed and washed the dishes. "This, at least, I learned at home," he said. "My mother was very precise about cleanliness."

"We always had a maid for such things," Ezra said.

"Was your family wealthy, in France?"

"In Tours, there were always girls so poor that they were willing to work for Jews," he said. "I know my mother didn't pay them much, and she and my grandmother did most of the work. By the time we moved to Paris, my father was more successful, and we had a proper maid who cleaned, and a girl who took care of my grandmother as she got older."

Ezra took a cloth and began drying the dishes that Silas washed. "And your family?" he asked.

"When I was young, we lived very simply, but gradually I see my father must have brought in more money. There was enough to send me to school, and to have a woman come and teach my sister needlework and music. I never felt poor, or rich either. It was only when I was on my own that I realized the value of money."

It was so sweet, standing beside Ezra over the sink, and Silas wondered if his parents had ever felt this way. Had they been in love? They must have been, once. By the time he was old enough to notice, his father had begun to pay more attention to the bottle than to his wife, and his mother had grown weary and old before her time.

Ezra turned and placed a damp hand on Silas's arse. "I have been waiting for you all day," he said, as he squeezed the muscles there.

"While I have been working," Silas said, with his nose up in the air. He handed the last wet dish to Ezra to dry.

Ezra put it down on the counter and pulled Silas close for a kiss. Ezra had not shaved that morning, and his cheeks were rough. The feel of them sent shivers through Silas's body.

"Your lips taste of that artichoke dip," Silas said, when they released.

"You are my artichoke and I must peel you away to get to your delicious center," Ezra said, as he began undoing Silas's flies. With a tug, he had Silas's trousers and his undershorts down. Silas's cockstand popped out, but Ezra flipped him around so that he was facing the now empty table.

Silas bent forward, raising his arse up, and he felt so wanton in that moment, like a bitch in heat about to be mounted.

Ezra grabbed a container of oil and pushed a slick finger into Silas's arse, which he accepted willingly. His cock and bollocks were pressed against the table, and Ezra moved his legs farther apart. Then Ezra was inside him, pushing forward, past the starburst of pain that had Silas catch his breath and whimper.

"I will make it better, mon cher," Ezra said, as he pushed forward slowly. Soon Silas felt that magnificent fullness, as he and Ezra were connected through a rod of flesh, iron, and emotion.

Ezra flexed his muscular hips and pulled back from Silas, leaving only his tip inside, then pushed forward again. In and out, in a slow, sensuous manner, as Silas's heart ticked and sweat pooled at his neck and under his arms.

It was hard for Silas to think clearly, but he recognized how useful all those muscles of Ezra's became as the boxer gripped his upper arms and flexed his buttocks to push forward and then pull back. The pressure on Silas's cock against the table grew unbearable and his bollocks contracted. The glory filled him and he spent on the polished wood.

Ezra kept going, though, whispering in French, then cursing, then finally groaning and spending inside Silas's arse.

He slumped against Silas for a moment or two, their bodies merging on a tide of sweat and desire. "I am like an animal with you," Ezra said. "My body is no longer my own, it has its desires and urges."

"And I am your mate," Silas said as Ezra backed away, and Silas could turn to face him. "We are two lions on the plains of Africa. We hunt, we eat, and we fuck."

Ezra laughed. "I want to fuck you in each room of this house," he said. "And when we have completed the circuit I want to start it again, and then again."

"You will have no argument from me." Silas leaned forward and kissed him.

Then Ezra reached under his buttocks with one strong arm and lifted him, and wrapped the other around Silas's back. Without even a stumble, he carried Silas, his trousers still wrapped around his shoes, up the stairs to the second floor.

He deposited Silas on the floor in the bedroom and slapped his arse once after he had his balance.

They fucked twice more that night, both of them naked as the day they were born, and then slept long into the morning.

Silas woke comfortably in Ezra's embrace. But he worried how long this domesticity could last. What if the judge refused to dismiss the charges against Ezra? What if instead he was held over on charges of sodomy? And if Silas himself was implicated, and arrested?

He squirmed out of Ezra's embrace without waking him, and walked to the toilet. He did his business, then sat there for a few moments longer, his mind full of all the things that could conspire to keep him and Ezra apart, to perhaps even ruin his life. Then with a sigh that made him feel at least fifty years older, he rose and returned to the bedroom.

Ezra was already awake, and their stomachs grumbled nearly in unison. They dressed quickly and stepped outside. The street was so quiet Silas was alarmed. "Is something wrong?" he asked.

"Everyone is at shul," Ezra said. "Today is our Sabbath. But do not worry, I know a restaurant outside this neighborhood that serves breakfast."

He led Silas down one street and then another, until they had left the Jewish neighborhood behind. "You are very quiet this morning," Ezra said. "Does this area bother you?"

Silas shook his head. "Just worried about the future."

"I am worried, too," Ezra said. "But we cannot change anything that will happen on Monday. Instead I think we must enjoy the time we have together."

He smiled, and Ezra's heart skipped a beat. At the restaurant, he noticed that Ezra asked for an extra helping of potatoes in place of his bacon. "You don't eat pork?" he asked after the server had left.

"I tried, when I was younger," Ezra said. "In rebellion. I ate sausages, bacon, and ham, but I never developed a taste for it." He shrugged. "Some habits lie deep."

They talked over breakfast, and Silas marveled again at the direction his life had taken. From rough sucking or fucking in alleys to this sweet domesticity. He did not know how long it would last, but he was determined to relish it while it did.

After breakfast they took a long walk, and Silas was surprised to see Luke on the street, play-boxing with another boy. "Do you live nearby?" he asked.

"This is my school," Luke said, pointing to the warehouse behind him. "Even though it is Saturday and there are no classes, I came here to see my friends."

"And to box with them?" Silas asked.

Luke nodded. "Though our teacher left and none of us really know what to do."

"Let me show you," Ezra said. They walked into the courtyard of the warehouse, and Silas saw several ragged young boys and girls peering at books and practicing their writing.

"Here, you shouldn't hold your pencil like that," Silas said to a girl of about ten. She was gripping it like the handle of a stirring spoon. He sat beside her and took the pencil, then held it between his second and third finger, steadying it with his thumb.

"Teacher showed us that, but it's hard," the girl said.

While Silas sat with her and a few of her friends, coaxing them through their letters, Ezra gathered a group of boys to demonstrate the proper stance in boxing. Silas and Ezra spent several hours there until the children began to leave, either to work or head home for meals.

"I enjoyed that," Ezra said as they walked away. "It felt good to be able to pass on what I have learned."

"You could return here," Silas said. "Luke said that his teacher was gone. And maybe you can train another to become a new Hammer."

"I don't know that I can do that much," Ezra said. "But it would give me some purpose while I wait to return to the ring."

As they walked, Ezra said, "I have realized many things since that night when the police came for me at New Cross," he said, as they walked. "I have been selfish for a long time. Focused only on my body and my skill, on making money and becoming successful."

"Some might call that self-preservation. You told me that originally you learned to box to be able to fight against boys who sought to torment you because of your religion."

"And I did. But I let it take control of me. I let my father force me into marriage with Rebecca when I knew it was not fair to either of us. I agreed to come to London with her because I thought it would be easier to find men to have sex with and keep my secrets."

"And did that work out?"

"Well, I met you," Ezra said. "But only in these last days have I realized how much you mean to me. How you have stood by me, and recruited your friends, and Pemberton. That is the sign of a true connection – one I never felt with Rebecca, or with any other man."

"I feel the same way," Silas said. "Before I met you, I was happy to be a butterfly, flitting from one man to another. When I considered that I might lose you, it felt so much worse than losing anyone else in the past. Worse, even, than my father sending me away and leaving behind my family."

"We shall both have to work to make sure that we can stay together," Ezra said.

They feasted that night on leftover chicken and hard-boiled eggs, and Silas was happy simply to cuddle with Ezra in bed.

Sunday morning he woke to church bells, and thought about following their sound to a place where he could ask God to look after him and Ezra. But everything he remembered from church as a child condemned the two of them for their acts. So he turned on his side and went back to sleep, trusting the world rather than asking for divine intervention.

When he finally awoke for good, he stepped over to the window and looked out at the street. The neighborhood was alive again with peddlers on the street and children playing as their mothers gossiped. Ezra showed Silas a back entrance to the house which led to an alley overhung with trees, so they could come and go without making a show for the neighbors.

It all felt like a fairy story, though Silas knew that there was danger outside the door. Despite the work that everyone had done, Ezra could still be convicted, sentenced, and sent to prison. What would happen to his accounts, his house? Would Silas be evicted, losing not just the man of his heart but the house he had already begun to think of as home?

Chapter 36

An Excellent Pair

Silas

Silas woke early on Monday morning, used the toilet, and washed himself. He could not help thinking about what the day would bring, and all the optimism Ezra had encouraged in him faded away as he toasted a few slices of leftover bread from Friday night and made himself a pot of tea. He was eating when Ezra came downstairs in his undershirt and shorts, his hair sleep-tousled.

"Is this to be your regular routine?" he asked, as he poured himself a cup of tea. He sat across from Silas and took a piece of buttered toast from his plate.

"As long as I continue to work," Silas said. "Have you forgotten the significance of this date? The hearing to dismiss the charges against you is scheduled for this morning."

"I thought of little else all night," Ezra said. "Worrying that it will not go my way."

Silas knew it was important for him to push aside his own worries and help Ezra feel better. "I have faith in Antony Wigton and Richard Pemberton," Silas said. "And in my own work, finding material for them to take to court."

"Your law has not always been right for my people. For Jews, or inverts."

"You are the one who told me to be optimistic," Silas said. "To enjoy the time we have together."

"And what if they take me back to gaol from the courtroom?"

"They won't," Silas said, though he wasn't sure. "You are on bail. That means you are free until your trial. Today's hearing is merely to assess the charges against you in light of the information Rebecca provided to the police."

He leaned over and kissed Ezra's grizzled cheek. "You are to meet Wigton at his office. Will you be able to get there on your own?"

Ezra frowned. "I have made my way in London since I arrived. No need to treat me like a mother hen with a chick."

Silas finished the last of his toast and wiped his mouth. "Then I will see you in court," he said.

He fretted the whole way to Pemberton's office, and could hardly concentrate on the work in front of him until it was time to accompany Pemberton to court. Outside, in the flurry of bewigged barristers and harried clerks, he spotted Ezra approaching, in his best suit, accompanied by Wigton.

Once again Silas was surprised at how quickly things went. Pemberton presented his case, and there was no argument from the crown's prosecutor, so the charges were dismissed and Ezra was a free man. There was no mention made of his sexual condition.

Silas felt as if someone had inflated a balloon inside him. All the fear he had felt since the time of Ezra's arrest floated up through him and out his mouth, leaving him with a curious feeling of lightness.

There were still obstacles to be overcome. Would Ezra be able to box again, either in London or out in the countryside? Would he have to relocate to France? Would Ezra have enough money to support both of them in the house in Hackney? If not, what would Silas do?

None of that mattered, though. Ezra was free and the specter of imprisonment that had loomed over him had been lifted. Everything else would happen as it would.

When Ezra was led out to have the bail restrictions lifted, Silas made to rise, but a finger from Pemberton told him to remain. A short time later, another barrister rose to address charges against Bertie Greenbaum and his enforcer Alfie Gibbons. The two cases were yoked together; Greenbaum was charged with running a betting operation, and Gibbons for the fatal punch to Nathan Walpert. Despite Greenbaum's assurance that he had ample funds to secure his release, the judge would not grant either of them bail, and they were both remanded to Queen's Bench Prison.

Only then did Pemberton rise, and Silas followed him outside.

"Do you need to meet with Mr. Curiel?" Pemberton asked.

"No, he said that once he was free, he would return to Hackney, and I will see him there this evening."

He turned to Pemberton. "That was so easy. Are all cases dismissed so simply?"

"I did not feel comfortable telling you about this until after today's hearing," Pemberton said. "Saturday morning I received a message from Gerard Houghton, who was being held in gaol. He was caught in flagrante on Friday evening, and since this was his second offense, he was worried that he would have to serve gaol time."

"What did you do?"

"I referred him to Antony Wigton, who met with him and convinced him that by offering up the information he had about Walpert's murder, he might gain his freedom."

"As I recall, he was reluctant to do anything that would bring him back into police orbit," Silas said. "But I guess his urges were too strong."

"They can be difficult to master," Pemberton said, and Silas wondered once more about his employer. He was circumspect about his private life, and even after some time in the office Silas knew nothing about how he satisfied those urges himself.

They walked past the old woman and the hearth and outside. The weather had warmed a bit, so at least there was no punishingly cold wind.

"Houghton apparently had placed the odd bet with Greenbaum, and he knew the bookie could be a formidable opponent. He didn't want to get on the man's wrong side, until he had the choice of gaol."

"I am still angry that he put Ezra through so much."

"In the course of time working with me, Mr. Warner, you will learn that generally witnesses do what is best for them, not necessarily what is right or even within the law." He slapped Silas on the back. "In any case, Antony Wigton arranged everything. Because the prosecutor already had another suspect in custody for the murder, along with an eye-witness, he was willing to discharge the charges against Ezra quickly."

"What will happen to Houghton?"

"He has been strongly cautioned to keep his cock in his pants and his mouth to himself," Pemberton said. "And that if he is arrested a third time, things will not go well for him, no matter what information he has to trade."

"I feel sorry for him," Silas said. "There have been a few occasions when I might have come to the attention of the police, but I was lucky."

"And now you have a handsome man by your side, and a house where you can have your way with each other," Pemberton said. "I envy you that."

Silas was emboldened to ask, "Do you ever wish you could find a man of your own?"

"I am past those days," Pemberton said. "Now I am happy to observe handsome young men, in art and in the flesh, and satisfy myself."

Silas hoped that he would never come to that point. He wanted to be as old as Pemberton and still randy as a goat, particularly if he could have Ezra by his side.

Ezra began to visit the Ragged School each day. While the children were in class, he exercised in the yard, and then began to offer the same lessons in gymnastics and self-defense that had been previously offered, and found several young men he could mentor as boxers.

A week later, a letter arrived from Rebecca. She was settled in her father's house and had made arrangements for the Bet Din, the court that would grant them a divorce, shortly after the new year.

"How do you feel about that?" Silas asked.

"I am happy, but frightened," Ezra said. "Among my people, all I must do to divorce Rebecca is to announce that to her, once we have the blessing of the panel of rabbis. But she can be vindictive, and I worry that she will expose my nature to her family, and mine."

"Must there be someone to blame?"

Ezra shrugged. "I don't know. But this afternoon I spoke with the promoters at the New Cross arena, and was advised to wait until the new year to consider returning to the ring."

"How do you feel about that?" Silas asked.

"I don't mind taking some time off," Ezra said. "With Bertie Greenbaum in gaol, there is some infighting among other bookmakers, and men are not betting as much as they have in the past. And there is much buzz in the arena, apparently. Most of it to do with my strength, and the possibility that I could have killed Walpert had I wanted to."

"Did you ever hear the story about the tailor who said he had killed seven at one blow?"

Ezra shook his head. "Someone you knew?"

"No, one of the fairy stories I heard as a boy. The tailor killed seven flies with one swipe of his fist, and then bragged about it. A giant assumed he was talking about killing men, and challenged him to a fight."

"Which the giant must have won."

Silas shook his head. "No, the tailor was a clever man and he kept managing to best the giant. I can't recall the ending other than that the tailor lived happily ever after."

"Was there a point?"

"My father made it sound like the tailor was a braggart, and needed to be punished, but my mother insisted that the story was about how brains could triumph over strength."

"And you, what do you think?"

"If I were writing the story, I would have the tailor and the giant fall in love," Silas said. "Nothing can beat the combination of brains and strength."

"Then we shall be an excellent pair," Ezra said.

Author's Note

Regular readers of my fiction will know that I like to make connections to my real life. It helps me feel more connected to the characters sometimes. Steve Levitan in my golden retriever mysteries shares his last name with my great-grandmother, and Steven is my middle name. Nathan Walpert could be a distant relation of mine, were he real. My great-great-grandmother on another side of the family was Esther Rachel Walpert. She was one of seven children, including two boys. Though she was living in Lithuania at the time of this book, she could have had cousins who emigrated!

This is the third in my series of Ormond Yard Romantic Adventures, which began with *The Gentleman and the Spy* and the way that Magnus and Toby come together. It was followed by *The Lord and the Frenchman*, which is John's and Raoul's story. I like to tie the books to historical actions during the time period. The Suez Canal deal did take place around this time, and provided a useful red herring for the plot. John's broadsides also recognize current events of the time.

I am grateful to librarian Chris Caspar for helping me discover sources to answer particular questions. I appreciate the research of

Author's Note

Sarah Elizabeth Cox in Victorian boxing, which has proved very helpful. Ezra's life is based in part on that of Daniel Mendoza, a prominent English prizefighter in the 1780s and 90s, and also a Jew of Sephardic origin.

I used the British Museum's online exhibit, "Jewish Britain: A History in 50 Objects," to learn about Jewish life at the time. *The Dictionary of Victorian London* was also very useful, particularly in its descriptions of the Queen's Bench Prison. And the section from *Cassell's Family Magazine* on Barrister's Clerks helped me understand what Silas's work would be like.

Thanks for reading! I'd love to stay in touch with you. Subscribe to one or more of my newsletter or Gay Mystery & Romance and Golden Retriever Mysteries and I promise I won't spam you!

Follow me at Goodreads to see what I'm reading, and my author page at Facebook where I post news and giveaways.

Looking for something new to read? Neil has a series just for you!

Author of over 50 romance and mystery novels and short story collections. **Neil's entire catalog of books are here:** www.mahubooks.com

Acknowledgments

I'm delighted that readers have embraced my men of Ormond Yard. I've left open several men in this book who could have their own stories—Richard Pemberton, Gerard Houghton, and Luke O'Shea. I hope you'll let me know whose story you would like to see next! There is also another book in the works, set in Tangier at the same time as these books, but that manuscript has been kicking my butt for a while and I'm not sure when it will be ready. Part of the problem is that it started out to feature Magnus and Toby in supporting roles, but the protagonist has told me he doesn't need their help. We'll see.

Beta readers Andy Jackson and Bob Kman helped identify errors in the manuscript, though any that remain are my fault.

As usual, thanks go to my editor, Randall Klein, my assistant Stacey Ducker, and cover designer Kelly Nichols. Puppy kisses to Brody and Griffin, and of course to Marc, who makes it all possible.

About the Author

NEIL S. PLAKCY is the author of over fifty mystery and romance novels, including the best-selling golden retriever mysteries and the highly acclaimed *Mahu* series, a three-time finalist for the Lambda Literary Awards. His stories have been featured in numerous venues, including the Bouchercon anthology Florida Happens and Malice Domestic's Murder Most Conventional and several Happy Homicides collections.

He is a professor of English at Broward College in South Florida, where he lives with his husband and their rambunctious golden retrievers.

His website is www.mahubooks.com.

www.ingramcontent.com/pod-product-compliance
Lightning Source LLC
LaVergne TN
LVHW012014060526
838201LV00061B/4296